MOP, MOONDANCE, AND THE NAGASAKI KNIGHTS

MOP, MOONDANCE, AND THE NAGASAKI KNIGHTS

Walter Dean Myers

HARCOURT BRACE & COMPANY

Orlando Atlanta Austin Boston San Francisco Chicago Dallas New York
Toronto London

This edition is published by special arrangement with Bantam
Doubleday Dell Books for Young Readers, a division of Bantam
Doubleday Dell Publishing Group, Inc.

Grateful acknowledgment is made to Bantam Doubleday Dell
Books for Young Readers, a division of Bantam Doubleday Dell
Publishing Group, Inc., New York, for permission to reprint
Mop, Moondance, and the Nagasaki Knights by Walter Dean
Myers. Copyright © 1992 by Walter Dean Myers.

Printed in the United States of America

ISBN 0-15-307549-X

2 3 4 5 6 7 8 9 10 025 99 98 97

For Samantha

"**Y**ou think they're going to be sad?" Moon-dance asked. We were in Lincoln Park watching his sailboat turn in small circles in the middle of Lincoln Park lake.

"Mom said it happened a long time ago," I said. "She said that it happened to their grandparents but they all know about it."

"Wars are bad," Moondance said.

He looked sad. That's the way Moondance is. Whenever he hears about something bad happening he gets sad. We were all excited about the three Little League teams that were coming from other countries to play in the United States. One team was from Mexico, one was from France, and the other one was from Nagasaki, Japan.

Mom showed us on a map that Mexico touched the United States. France was all the way across the Atlantic Ocean in Europe. You had to go east to get to Europe, and west, over the Pacific Ocean, to get to Japan. Mom told us that during the Second World War the United States dropped an atomic bomb on Nagasaki. That was what made Moondance sad.

"I hope we don't ever have another war," Moondance said. "And I hope we never have a bomb dropped on us."

"I hope that nobody gets a bomb dropped on them," I said. "Mom says if we get to know all the kids from other countries, we won't want to drop bombs on them when we get older."

"I don't want to drop any bombs on them now," Moondance said.

That was right. Moondance didn't want to drop bombs on anybody, and I didn't want to drop bombs on anybody, and no kid I ever knew wanted to drop bombs on another kid. I couldn't figure out who would want to do it.

A breeze had pushed the boat to the middle of the lake, where it had sat for almost forever, or at least half an hour. The boat just turned around and around without coming to the shore. Moondance was hoping a fish would come by and make some waves that would push the boat toward us.

"I don't think we're going to get my boat back either," Moondance said.

"Maybe Mop has some ideas," I said. "Here she comes now."

Moondance took a quick look at his boat and then at Mop.

"They're here!" Mop was walking toward us but

she still sounded out of breath, the way she does when she wants you to know that something is important. "I just saw them practicing!"

"All of them?" Moondance asked.

"I saw the Mexican guys and the team from Japan," Mop said. "But Sister Titi said the French team was here too. What are you guys doing?"

"Moondance's boat is in the middle of the lake," I said. "We're waiting until it comes over to one side, so we can get it."

Mop put her hand up so that the sun wouldn't be in her eyes as she looked at Moondance's boat. "Suppose it doesn't come back?" she said.

"It'll come," Moondance said.

"How did they look?" I asked.

"I couldn't really tell," Mop said. "I didn't want to stare or anything. But I think they're pretty good."

"Better than us?" I said.

"How can they be better than us when we're the champions?" Mop asked.

"That's true," I said. We had won the championship last year in the very last game of the play-offs. Moondance had pitched that game and Mop had been the catcher.

"I don't think we should have to play to see who goes to Japan," Mop said. "Everybody said so."

"Mr. Treaster messed it up," Moondance said.

"My mom said he could mess up a flat rock."

Mop knelt by the edge of the lake and put her fingers in the water.

She was right about Mr. Treaster. That was the kind of guy he was. Take last summer for example. It looked like it was going to be a perfect summer and a perfect baseball season until Mr. Treaster started messing with everybody. But it turned out all right because we won the championship over his stupid Eagles and Mop got adopted, which was just about as good as winning the championship. Being adopted is really good. Me and Moondance were adopted the year before Mop, so we know all about it.

So we won the championship and then this skinny guy from the newspaper comes to see our coach. Our coach, by the way, is Mrs. Kennedy, Mop's new mom. Before she adopted Mop and became the coach of the team we used to call her by her first name, Marla. That was a cool name, but it wasn't the kind of name you called your coach. And Mop said she was still going to call her Mom no matter what we called her. Anyway, what the guy wants to do is to invite some teams from other countries to come and play the teams from Lincoln Park. The city council worked it out with some airline and three teams were invited to New Jersey. It's supposed to be some kind of a goodwill program so that we could learn to get along with kids from other countries, which is pretty cool.

Then some guy from Japan—he was really from Bayonne, but he was Japanese and I think his parents were from Japan—invited the Elks (that's us, the champions) to go over to Japan and play after our season was over. That was cool, too, but that's when Mr. Treaster got into it.

"We should play a tournament," he said. "The three teams that are coming over here and the best three American teams from last year. Then the American team with the best record goes to Japan."

Mr. Treaster's team is the Eagles. Most of the Eagles are pretty ugly. They're the biggest, ugliest twelve-year-old guys you've ever seen in your life. Everybody knew Mr. Treaster just wanted to get his team a chance to go to Japan. Everybody knew it, but we got stuck with the tournament anyway.

I wasn't sure I wanted to go to Japan, because to get there you had to fly in a plane. My mom said you had to fly for about a whole day. It wasn't like I was afraid to fly or anything, maybe just a little bit nervous, but not afraid. But I didn't like the idea that you had to fly over the Pacific Ocean. Say you didn't like to fly over the ocean but you were halfway there, right? You either had to fly the rest of the way or turn around and fly just as far back. I really wasn't that nervous about it though, because I'm just about the bravest guy I ever met.

Okay, I didn't want the Eagles to get to go in our place, either.

Oh, by the way, my name is T.J., and I'm the star of the Elks, which, like I said, is the name of our team.

"You ought to blow on your boat," Mop said. "Blow it over to one side."

"I can't blow that far," Moondance said.

"Mom said she's having tryouts Saturday," Mop said, checking a watch that hung on a cord around her neck. "I gotta go. Don't be late Saturday."

Mop started out of the park and we watched her go for a while and then I turned and saw that Moondance's boat was almost on the other side of the lake.

"Come on," Moondance said. "I'll race you to the other side."

Moondance knew I didn't like to race. That's because I run too fast for my heart. If your feet hit the ground faster than your heart beats, then your nose might start to bleed. That's why I ran slow and let Moondance get to the other side of the lake first. We got the boat and started home.

"You ready for baseball?" I asked him.

"I don't know," he said, lifting his shoulders the way he does sometimes. "I guess I'll find out Saturday."

Saturday was so hot you wouldn't even believe it. It was like the sun was right over us and squeezing out all its hot juices right down on us. You figure it was so hot nobody would start anything. But then Brian showed up.

"You know what your name should be?" Brian asked Mop.

"Don't start with me, Brian." Mop pushed her catcher's mask toward the back of her head. "I don't want to have to break your nose before the season begins."

"No, no," Brian said. "This is real. How come your name is Mop?"

"How come your name is Brian?" Mop asked.

" 'Cause my parents gave me that name," Brian said. "That's my real name. But that ain't your real name."

Which was true. The name that Mop had at the Dominican Academy, which is where she had been and where Moondance and I had been before we got adopted, was Olivia Parrish. That's what Mop stood for—Miss Olivia Parrish. And I knew just what Brian was going to say.

"Since you got adopted by Mrs. Kennedy, your new name should be Mok. Miss Olivia Kenn—"

He never got the whole "Kennedy" out. Mop flew across the infield and tackled him right there on the pitcher's mound. There was a loud *ooof* and Brian went flying backward. Sister Titi, also from the Academy, ran over to break it up.

It took Sister Titi, Mrs. Kennedy, and Joey DeLea to break the fight up. The rest of us were just standing around watching it. When Mop got up her shirt was bloody.

"That'll teach you to open your mouth, you squirm!" Mop yelled over her mother's arm.

"At least I ain't bleeding," Brian said. "Look at your shirt."

"Yes, you are." Evans, our center fielder, had this high voice like the chipmunks on television. "Look at your nose!"

We all looked at Brian's nose and saw a thin trickle of blood over his upper lip. Brian touched his face with a finger, saw the blood, and threw his glove down.

Mrs. Kennedy made Mop go to one side of the field and made Brian go to the other. Later he came over and asked us if he was right or not.

"Her name ain't Parrish anymore," he said. "She can't be Mop."

"Maybe not," Evans said. "But I'm not going to tell her."

Nobody else did, either.

Most of the team from last year was still there. Lo Vinh and Frank Law were playing in the senior league and there were two new kids. One was a short guy named Benny. The other was a tall, skinny kid named Gregory. Benny talked a lot, but Gregory didn't say anything. I watched as Sister Titi hit them some fly balls. Benny missed three balls in a row. He really had to run hard after them.

Then Titi hit some to Greg and he caught them easily. He ran right to where the ball was coming down, so it wasn't that hard for him.

"I think I'm going to call you Greg," Brian said. "Gregory's too long."

When it was my turn to catch fly balls I think the sun was just starting to go down. So the sun was shining on one part of the ball and the other half was in shadow. It was like I was trying to catch half a ball. Titi hit four balls to me. Two were too far away to catch. By the time I got to them they had already been taken over by gravity and fell to the ground. Once a ball is taken over by gravity you can't catch it no matter what happens. The other two hadn't been taken over by gravity yet and I almost caught both of them. That's not bad for the first day of tryouts.

Everybody tried out for all the positions and everybody made the team, which was good. "Are we going to have three girls on the team again?" Joey asked.

"Yes," Sister Titi said.

"That's why Mr. Treaster doesn't like us," Joey said. "Because we beat his Eagles and we've got three girls on our team."

"I'm sure he can find other reasons as well," Mrs. Kennedy said.

"Hey, I've got a name for you, Mrs. Kennedy," Brian said.

When he said that Mop took off her mask and got ready to fight again.

"Since your name is Mrs. Kennedy—M.K.—we'll call you Mack," Brian went on.

"You can call me 'Coach,'" Mrs. Kennedy said, stepping in front of Mop.

Mop took a look at her mother—a squinty-eyed look to see if she was mad. She wasn't. She told everyone to call her Coach.

Just when we got up to start hitting, guess who comes along? The Japanese team! I can't believe it, because the whole team is Japanese!

Coach was pitching them up and everybody got a turn to hit. You got ten swings each. Greg, one of the new kids, hit eight shots to the outfield. Mop got five pretty good shots and Brian put one over the fence.

"Not bad for a squirm, huh?" he said to Mop.

"Here's your reward," Mop said. She took out her gum and threw it to him. He swung at it and knocked it over the backstop.

I hit the ball seven times. Mostly they were foul, but one was too close to tell.

None of us looked over at the Japanese kids much, but when we did we saw that they were watching us. When we finished the tryouts Jennifer invited us all to her house. She went over to Benny and Gregory to make sure they would come.

"I'm busy," Greg said.

"What you going to do?" Jennifer asked. That was Jennifer, real nosy.

"What I do ain't none of your business," Greg said.

He gave Jennifer a real mean look and just started walking away. Coach called after him and told him not to forget that we were going to have a practice on Monday at four o'clock.

"Hey, Mop, you think I should have knocked him out?" Jennifer asked.

"Let's see how good he is first," Mop said.

Of the three girls on the team, Mop is the toughest, then Jennifer, and Chrissie isn't tough at all. I don't think Jennifer could have knocked out the new kid, though.

We went over and shook hands with the Japanese kids and they bowed to us and then we bowed to them and then some of our guys started laughing. The Japanese guys started laughing too. They looked like they were going to be okay.

When we got to Jennifer's house her mother had cupcakes and iced tea. I don't like iced tea. Cupcakes are okay, but not that great. Jennifer had a piano and right in the center of it was her trophy from last year. But you know who else was at Jennifer's house? One of the players from the French team!

"Don't say any secrets," Brian said.

"This is Claude," Jennifer's mother said.

At first I thought that Claude was a girl. He had eyes like a girl, with long eyelashes, and his hair was kind of long too.

"How are you feeling?" Claude said.

"Fine," Joey said.

"That is very good," Claude said.

Everybody thought that it was kind of cool that Claude could speak English and French, but I would have liked it better if the French kids only spoke French, because it would have seemed more like they were foreign. Claude said that most of them spoke English.

We sat around and talked a little and everybody took a good look at Claude and he took a pretty good look at us too.

After some more iced tea and some cupcakes we found out why we were invited over to Jennifer's house. Claude had gone into the other room to watch television and the coach made us all gather around.

"At the end of last year," she said, "we won the championship, which was good, but we also made a lot of friends."

"Is this going to be like a sermon?" Joey asked.

"A little," Coach said.

"That's good," Joey said. "I like that kind of speech."

"Well, I just want to say that this year we'll have

an opportunity to make even more friends," Coach said.

That was pretty good, because the way I figured it, you never knew when you were going to run out of friends.

"And though I want to win," Coach went on, "I think making friends might even be more important than winning."

"I don't think so," Brian said.

Some of the games we played were going to be tournament games and some were going to be exhibition games. This was so that everybody would have a good chance to see the teams from other countries play. Then the American team that won the most tournament games would get to go to Japan.

"Suppose everybody wins the same amount of games?" Evans asked.

"That's not very likely," Coach said. "But if they do, then everybody will be a winner. But the important thing to remember is that we're here to have fun."

The first game of the tournament was between the Eagles and the Mexican team. Naturally we all went to see it.

The Mexican team was called "Los Hermanos." A woman in the stands told Mop that it meant "The Brothers." I don't think they were really brothers, though, because they didn't look like one another.

The Eagles were up first. They had been big last

year but they were even bigger this year. The Mexican pitcher was kind of fat with a round chest and short legs. He looked jerky when he pitched, but he could throw really fast. Just the same, the Eagles hit the ball hard, but wherever they hit the balls the Mexican guys got them.

"Soon as they get the ball they're ready to throw it too," Brian said.

"They're good!" Moondance said.

"And they're playing our game," Coach said.

I looked at her and she had this big smile on her face. I didn't see what was so funny about that.

Then the Mexican team got up and scored three runs. They didn't hit the ball hard, but they got down to first base really fast. Once a ball went right back to the Eagles' pitcher, Chris Baber. It just rolled slowly, but it went right to him. Chris waited until the ball got to him, then picked it up and threw it to first. Too late.

"Hustle it up, Chris! Hustle it up!" Mr. Treaster was yelling.

When the Eagles got up again they went out one, two, three. Rocky hit a long drive, but their left fielder caught it just in front of the fence. The whole Eagles bench had jumped up when Rocky hit the ball. But when the Mexican guy caught it they all sat down and you could tell they were thinking about losing.

"Look at Mr. Treaster," Moondance said.

I looked over and saw Mr. Treaster leaning against the fence with his arms folded. I couldn't see his face too clear from where I was standing, but I figured he was looking mean. That was the way he was. He wasn't very nice when he was losing.

Every time the Mexican team got up they got a few runs. Every time the Eagles got up they got nothing. Mr. Treaster had a clipboard and he kept writing things down on it. The way I figured it, he would have his whole pad filled up pretty soon.

Okay, so the Mexican guys won the first game of the tournament. I thought that was okay, because it wasn't the regular season or anything like that. But after the game I saw Mr. Treaster come over to talk to Coach and start waving his hands around and that kind of thing. Mop was standing nearby and came over to tell us what Mr. Treaster had said.

"He said the Mexican kids look older than us," she said. "Mom said that she didn't think so."

"You can't go around calling the coach 'Mom,'" Brian said. "You got to call her Coach like the rest of us."

"Then he asked *Mom*," Mop said, giving Brian a little look out of the corner of her eye, "if she wanted him to send her anything from Japan when the Eagles go."

We all started figuring if we had a chance to go to Japan. It was between us, the Hawks, and the Eagles. We had won last year, but the Eagles were good. The Hawks weren't bad either.

"And the Eagles already lost one game," Jennifer said.

Which was true. We had to play that afternoon, and if we won we would be higher than the Eagles. The way I figured, with me rested over the winter and everything, we had to win.

We lost.

The Nagasaki Knights were pretty lucky and we were pretty unlucky. The first thing that happened was that Joey DeLea, who was pitching, walked the first four Japanese guys in a row. He said it was hard to pitch to the Japanese guys because they were so short. He was right too. Some of them were almost as short as Joey and it's really hard to pitch to him.

I played in center field and I played it so good it was like being wonderful. Everybody thought the first ball that got hit my way was going to go right through to the fence. That was because it was some shot. You could hear the bat go *whack!* and that ball came flying out to me like nobody's business. It came closer and closer and I just watched it. I didn't move, not even a muscle. Then, at the last minute, I jumped out of the way so it wouldn't hit me, and at the same time I knocked it down. Then I picked it up and threw it in to Mike, who was playing third base. It was the kind of play they show you on the news sometimes.

"So why didn't you catch it!" Mop started screaming at me when we got back to our dugout.

"I did catch it, stupid!" I said. "Wake up!"

"It hit the ground first!" Mop was yelling.

"Did you think it was going to fly in the air forever?"

Sometimes Mop isn't too bright. She started to show me how I had knocked the ball down and everything. I *knew* how I had done it, she didn't have to show me.

Greg and Benny, the new kids, didn't start. But when Greg was on the bench he wouldn't even watch the game. Coach told him he had to watch it so that he would know what to do if he came in. He watched it sort of, but not too close.

"Hey, Mop, doesn't Greg remind you a little of the kids at the Academy?"

"Yeah, a little," Mop said. She looked down the bench at Greg. "Just a little."

When we got up the Knights' pitcher—his name was Yosho—didn't walk anybody. He just pitched strikes, so you had to swing. Chrissie struck out. Then Mike Nieto struck out and Mop hit a fly ball for the third out. Not too good.

They got up again with the score four to nothing. Joey only walked one batter, but he hit two. That loaded the bases up again and the next guy hit a ground ball to third base. It went right through Mike's legs. They got three more runs and that made it seven to nothing.

Brian was up first for us and hit a little ground ball right to their first baseman. He was mad, but that's the way it goes sometimes. Coach put her arm around Brian and he pushed it off his shoulders.

Then Joey got up and took three hard swings and missed all of them.

"Don't overswing like Joey," Coach told Moondance. "Take the first pitch."

I knew that "taking" a pitch meant you didn't swing at it. Moondance got up, looked at the pitcher, and shook his bat as if he were really going to take a good swing. Then he let the ball go by.

"Strike one!" That's what the umpire called out.

The next pitch was too low to hit.

"Strike two!"

Coach had explained that sometimes an umpire makes mistakes. That was a mistake.

Then Moondance swung and got a *click!* hit into right field. It wasn't a great hit that goes *whack!*, but it was okay.

Jennifer was up next and she hit the first pitch right back to the pitcher. The guy caught the ball for the third out, put it on the ground, and ran off. The Japanese team looked pretty good too.

By the time I got up in the third inning we were

nine runs behind. Their pitcher wound up and threw a ball that was a little high. I swung at it and it almost went over their second baseman's head, but he jumped up and caught it.

"T.J., that ball was nearly over your head," Coach said. "Why did you swing at it?"

I don't know what she was talking about. If that ball had been a little higher it probably would have been over the guy's glove and I would have had a hit.

Anyway, we lost twelve to nothing. Coach said it was the first-game jitters.

We all thought that the three foreign teams were going to kill everybody, but then the Hawks beat the French team. The French team was called Les Cavaliers. On one guy on their team the *C* from Cavaliers was on his back where it was supposed to be, but the *s* was all the way under his arm.

After the game some of the coaches got together and our team stood around the water fountain. Sister Titi was trying to get us to go talk to the Mexican team, but nobody wanted to. Then this guy from the French team came over to us. I think they talk a lot on the French team.

"Would you enjoy lunch with us?" this guy asked Evans.

"Nope," Evans said. Then he got his glove and started home.

Everybody on the team was going home and I

saw Coach give us a look. She had given us that talk about making friends and everything, so I told the French kid we could go to lunch with him if he wanted.

Actually it was past lunchtime, so Mop thought maybe we would just go for a soda. I would have liked to go for a slice of pizza, but Mop was the only one with money, so we decided to go for the soda.

"This is my friend, Andre," Stefan said. That's what kind of names they had. Names like Stefan and Andre and Claude. I guess they were okay names if you were used to them. Anyway, none of us laughed at their names.

"My name is T.J.," I said. "And this is Mop and this is my brother, Moondance."

"Moondance?" Andre said. Only, he said it like "Moondawnce."

"Moondawnce, Touché, and Moop," Stefan said.

"It's not Moop, it's Mop! You know, like you mop a floor." Mop made movements as if she were mopping.

"Oh." That's what the French kid said.

I didn't know how we were going to play baseball against these guys, but it wasn't going to be easy to talk to them.

The French team was really cool. No matter what happened they never yelled and they never got mad. If something happened they just let it happen. I liked that.

Stefan missed three ground balls in a row. When the fourth ball came to him he gave it a kick and it went right over to first base. Two Hawks scored, but they got the guy at first base. When I got home after the game I told my dad about how cool the French team was.

"That's because they don't know the object of the game," my dad said. "If you don't want to win you shouldn't play."

That was his idea. If you wanted to win, then you would win. If you didn't want to win you would lose. That's why he had me and Moondance out in the park practicing after the Hawks beat the French team. Mr. Griffin, the coach of the Hawks, was still putting their equipment in their bags. I was hoping he would leave before Dad started hitting fly balls to me.

"Okay, you catch the ball as you step forward with your left foot," Dad was saying. "Then you throw it. Got that?"

I nodded. It was always a good thing to agree with Dad when he gave you one of his talks. If you didn't agree with him he'd just keep on giving you more of a lecture until you did agree.

I went to the outfield and turned around. Dad looked like he was a thousand miles away. Moondance was in left field and Dad hit the first ball to him.

It was the highest ball I had ever seen in my entire life. The ball almost disappeared. I looked at Moondance and he was hitting his glove with his fist. The ball took forever to come down and you could hear it as it hit Moondance's glove. *Whop!*

Moondance took his glove off and shook his hand. It must have really hurt when he caught the ball, even with the glove on.

Then Dad hit me the ball. I watched it go up, up, until it almost disappeared, then it started coming down. I hit my glove with my fist just the way Moondance did. The ball hit really hard. It wasn't so much of a *whop!* as it was a *whup!*

I turned around to see what it had hit and saw the ball bounce over the fence. You know what I thought about? If a bug had been crawling along under the ground and that ball hit right over him

◆ 23

he would have thought it was an earthquake or something.

"Didn't you see the ball?" Dad had come all the way to the outfield.

"Yeah."

"Then why didn't you catch it?" he asked.

"Because I missed it," I said. I thought he had seen that.

We stayed out for about half an hour and Dad just got madder and madder. The wind kept blowing the ball right to Moondance. I figured that if it was blowing the ball to Moondance it had to be blowing it *away* from me. Dad didn't figure it.

It made me feel a little sad that he wanted me to catch the ball all the time. Nobody caught the ball all the time. If you caught the ball all the time nobody would ever win a game and it wouldn't be any fun to play.

"I think Dad said a bad word," Moondance said later when we were in our room. "He was telling Mom how he was hitting a ball to us."

"I don't think he likes me that much," I said. "I think he wants a kid that can really play ball good."

"You going to practice some more?" Moondance asked.

"Nope."

That was my big problem, practicing. I didn't catch very well and so when I practiced I kept missing the ball. It didn't make any sense to practice not catching, I could already do that. Especially if it was just going to get Dad mad. The thing I had to do was to wait until I could catch the ball and then practice.

Mop asked me and Moondance if we wanted to go to her house and see her new turtle, and we said we did. On the way over to her house Mop and Moondance were talking about comics and stuff like that, but I was practicing in my mind. I saw a program on television where this guy in ancient China was practicing how to shoot a bow and arrow in his mind and then he got to be great at hitting the bull's-eye. I thought about catching the ball in my mind, but then I started thinking about missing it so I began to talk about comics.

The turtle was really small and Mop said she didn't like it.

"How come?" Moondance asked.

"Mostly 'cause it doesn't do anything," Mop said.

We watched it for a while and she was right. It didn't do anything but stay in one spot. We poked it a little to see if it would move, but it just pulled its head in.

"Maybe it doesn't like to do anything," I said.

"It could be sick or something," Mop said.

Which was true. We took it out of the bowl she kept it in and put it on Mop's bed and it crawled a little, then stopped. I wondered what it was thinking about.

"I think," Mop said, "that we're going to have to win the tournament."

"How come?" Moondance asked.

"Because if we start losing a lot of games, then we're going to have to do a lot of other good-doing stuff," Mop said. "Before you know it they'll have us holding hands and singing songs and stuff to show how we don't mind losing."

"I don't think we can beat the Mexican team," I said.

"Well, we better beat the Eagles and the Hawks so we can go to Japan," Mop said. "I think everybody's going to be on our case if we don't win."

"Maybe," I said. Mop's turtle had started moving again. "After we won the tournament last year a lot of people talked about it. But Coach said it wasn't that important to win."

"Maybe," Mop said. "But Mr. Treaster said we were a bunch of ragamuffin players. He said we couldn't win again."

Mop was sounding more and more like Dad. I knew what she meant. She meant that she wanted to win. That's the way Mop was.

"What's your turtle's name, Mop?"

"I think I'm going to call him Scud," Mop said. " 'Cause he's slow as a Scud missile."

"He doesn't look like much," Moondance said.

"That's because I haven't shown him any moves yet," Mop said.

She threw a karate kick at Moondance and he blocked it. Then they went through some karate moves while Scud and I sat on the bed and watched. Anyway, I watched.

I didn't care that much if we won or if we didn't win. I wanted to win, but it wasn't like I was going to absolutely positively cross my heart and die a purple death if I didn't win. That's the way I felt sitting on the bed in Mop's house. The next day everything changed.

The next morning was really cloudy, but the weather guy said it wasn't going to rain. There were still a lot of clouds in the sky and people were wearing jackets to the park. A very round, sort of pinkish man from the French embassy or something like that had come to see the French team play. One of the men who worked in the park played the "Star-Spangled Banner" on a record player and everybody stood up. Then he played the French national anthem on the record player. Coach said the French national anthem is called the "Marseillaise." Everybody stood up for that too.

Then the game started. It was the Eagles against the French team. No contest. Rocky was pitching instead of playing first base the way he usually does. He was throwing the ball about twice as hard as he did last year. I couldn't believe he could throw the ball so hard.

He got the French team out pretty easily. Then the Eagles came up. They had two new kids on their team and you could tell they were twins. They were short and played with their shirts out. They spit a lot too. They could hit and catch and everything. At the end of two innings the score was eight to nothing in favor of the Eagles. At the end of four innings the score was nineteen to nothing.

"I don't think we're doing a lot to improve international relations," Coach said.

She was mad. The corners of her mouth were real tight.

"Why did you say that?" Evans asked.

"Because there's no reason to make the French team look so bad," Coach said.

At first the French team looked as if they didn't care, the way they always looked. But after a while, when they were in the field a long time, they began to look miserable. The French coach's name was Monsieur LeBlanc, and he kept looking over at the guy from the French embassy. He was calling out to his team, but in French, and I didn't know what he was saying.

I looked at Stefan and saw that he had pulled his hat way down on his head. His hair was long and it stuck out over his ears.

"Look at old Treaster," Mop said.

"Just watch the game," Coach said.

I looked over at Mr. Treaster and he was really smiling and writing stuff down on his clipboard. He was having a nice time for himself. That really got me mad. The one thing I hate is when people enjoy making other people feel bad.

The other thing I hate is to see worms crawling across the road after it rains.

The final score of the game was the Eagles thirty-one and the French nothing.

After the game Coach went over to talk to Mr. Treaster and she came back even madder than when she went over.

"What happened, Mom?" Mop was as mad as her mother and she didn't even know why.

"In case of a tie he wants to use total runs to be the tiebreaker," she said.

So what that meant was that if we won as many games as the Eagles and they scored more runs than we did, then they would go to Japan. That's why they scored so many runs against the French team, she said. I don't think anybody liked that except Mr. Treaster and the Eagles.

You know who else didn't like it? Greg.

"He's a dog!" That's what Greg said.

"Those stupid Eagles didn't have to do that," I said. I had walked over and sat against the fence next to Greg.

"Don't be sitting next to me," Greg said.

I looked at him and he looked like he was mad, so I went back over and sat next to Moondance. Gregory was just weird. Every time I thought he was okay he would get mad.

Mop came over to me. I thought she had seen what happened with Greg. But she had something else to say.

"I'm coaching the French team," she said.

"You're coaching the French team?" I asked.

"Not the whole team," she said. "Just some of them. I just told them."

I felt pretty good about that. I felt pretty good about everybody being mad at Mr. Treaster and the Eagles. When everybody on a team feels the same way, it's nice. That's the way I felt until I got home. Dad had been thinking about baseball again.

Dad had played baseball in the major leagues. Not for a long time, but for a while. He had a scrapbook and everything.

"Do you like playing baseball?" he asked me. The very tip of his nose was shiny.

"Yep," I said. "Did you like playing baseball when you were my age?"

"Did I like . . . ?" He nodded. "When I was your age I just loved baseball. I used to go over to the park in the mornings and wait until the other kids showed up. Sometimes I would be there for an hour or so by myself."

"You didn't know when you were supposed to be there?"

"I knew . . . no, I mean, we didn't have a game scheduled. We just used to choose up sides. I just wanted to play every day."

"That's good," I said.

"Right. Look, T.J." Dad leaned forward. "Would you like to go to Japan and play baseball with your team?"

"Sure."

"Well, what do you think you have to do to help your team win?" he asked.

"Get a lot of hits and stuff," I said.

"Very good," he said. He wiggled around in his chair a little.

Just then Mom came in and sat on the bed. Usually she didn't come in when Dad and I were having a heart-to-heart talk. She sat on the edge of the bed and looked at Dad.

"I think your father thinks you should practice a little more," Mom said. "But sometimes he overdoes it just a little bit."

Mom had a smile on her face, but when I looked at Dad he wasn't smiling. In fact, he looked a little sad.

Mom kissed me, patted my hand, and then left.

"Your mother thinks I want you to work too hard at this baseball," Dad said. "What do you think?"

"I think I'm already pretty good," I said.

"You do?"

"Sure," I answered.

He gave me a funny look, as if he were surprised that I knew how good I was. Then he just nodded and stood up.

"Okay," he said. "Maybe . . . maybe your mother knows some things better than I do. She thinks you have problems talking to me. You think you would come and tell me if you had a problem?"

"With baseball?"

"With anything," Dad said.

"I think so," I said.

He didn't say anything else, just gave me this funny little smile that was almost not even a smile, and then he left. I didn't think I'd have any real problems, but I thought I'd try to think one up so that he wouldn't feel bad.

Later, after supper, the telephone rang. It was Mop. She wanted to know if I had been watching television. Mop isn't allowed to watch television during the week.

Then, in a whispery voice, she wanted to know if I would help her train the French kids. I said okay. I said it right out, like that. Yes! But what I was really thinking was that I wasn't going to train them to be as good as me.

After I hung up I thought about Mop not being able to watch television. Her mother said she was watching too much television, so Moondance and me started an experiment. We were going to watch as much television as possible to see what happened. Then we were going to see if anything bad happened to us. If something bad happened we'd know how much television was too much, so when somebody's parents said they were watching too much television we'd know what they were talking about.

Me and Moondance were in the park talking and watching a guy throw a Frisbee to a dog when Mop came up walking like a zombie.

"Don't shake me or anything," she said.

"How come?"

"I've got Scud under my hat," she said. She took off her baseball cap and there was her stupid turtle sitting right on the top of her head.

"What are you doing with him on your head?" I asked.

"Taking him out for a walk," Mop said.

"You should take him out for a run," Moondance said.

"What are you guys doing?" Mop asked. "Getting ready for the game this afternoon?"

"Thinking about what happened last night," I said.

"What happened?"

"First, Mom brings out these cheeseburgers and Cokes for supper," I said.

"Yeah?" Mop put the turtle down on the top of her sneaker.

"Then after supper she says she wants to have Family Meeting Time. Only, the way she's looking at Dad, I know he knows what the meeting is all about."

"So what was it all about?" Mop asked.

"She's going to have a baby," Moondance said.

"You're already official," Mop said. "Mom told me we're all officially adopted, so they can't send us back."

"She told us not to worry and stuff," I said. "Just to think about how nice it's going to be to have a baby sister or brother."

"I don't know why she wants to have another kid when she's got us," Moondance said.

"You sad?" Mop asked.

"A little," I said. That was true. Maybe even more than a little. Mom looked really happy when she was talking about having a baby.

"That's two things that have got me annoyed," Mop said. "That dumb Mr. Treaster messing with the French team and your mom having a baby. I don't care about her having a baby, but I don't like to see you guys sad."

"That's a pair of things," Moondance said. "I think that's what they call pair-annoyed."

"Could be," Mop said. "You think it's going to be a boy or a girl?"

I didn't know what it was going to be, but I hoped it wasn't going to be some stupid kid that was cute and smart and liked to go out and practice with Dad and everything.

We tried to get Mop's dumb turtle to run but it wouldn't. Mop said it was in training to be a statue and then got mad because me and Moondance didn't laugh. We weren't in a laughing mood. We just went home to rest for the game.

The game with the Hawks started at twelve o'clock. Moondance was pitching and he pitched good. *Phht! Phht! Phht!* He was throwing strikes. We scored one run in the first inning when Brian got a double and Joey hit a fly ball that fell right in between their shortstop and their second base. Both of those guys were looking at each other and the ball fell in between them. Brian came running around third base so fast, you couldn't even believe it.

The Hawks scored two runs in the third inning and I thought they were going to win. But when we got to the sixth inning and we were only losing two to one I knew we had a chance. The Hawks were first up and Coach had put in Mike to pitch. Moondance was pitching okay, but she wanted to give Mike a chance.

"I don't want Moondance to pitch a whole game yet," she said.

Moondance was sitting on the bench right next to me. Jennifer was playing third base. Chrissie was playing first, and Mop was catching, so we had all three of our girls in.

The first Hawk hit the ball straight up in the air. Mop got under it until she was just sure where it was coming down, then she threw the mask away and caught it. She's some neat ballplayer. Then the next guy walked. The third Hawk, a little kid named Ramon, hit a line drive right past Jennifer into left field. The guy on first came all the way around to third and Ramon stopped on second base.

"We're going to lose," Moondance said.

"Don't say that," Sister Titi said. She didn't even turn around and I didn't know she was listening.

Then the next guy on the Hawks hit a little ground ball back to Mike and he threw him out, but they scored another run on the play.

"We're going to lose," Moondance said. This time Sister Titi didn't say anything.

The next guy struck out, but we were down by two runs.

Okay, so the score is three to one and it's the last of the sixth. Sometimes when it's the last inning Coach goes around the dugout and talks to everybody. This time she was just sitting there and I figured maybe she was mad. She didn't even say anything when Evans threw a cup of water on Brian. Brian called Evans a stupid chipmunk.

"At least I ain't wet," Evans said.

"I'd rather be wet than a chipmunk," Brian said.

"Shut up!" Mop said.

Mop was up first and she struck out.

"I think you're blind!" Brian said as Mop came back to the bench.

Then Brian got up and struck out.

Joey DeLea was up next, but you could tell he didn't want to be up because he kept looking over at us.

"Joey, try a bunt," Coach said.

Joey had tried bunting in practice and missed every ball. But the first ball the Hawks' pitcher threw to him he bunted down the third-base line. It was perfect and he made it to first base.

Their third baseman got mad and kicked the ground. Then the new guy, Benny, was up, and Coach told him to bunt too. He bunted and the ball went down to the first baseman. The first baseman came in and got the ball and then turned around, but there wasn't anybody on first base to throw it to. So now we had two men on base.

"Who made a mistake?" Coach asked.

"The second baseman was supposed to cover first," Chrissie said.

"Right."

Mr. Treaster was sitting behind the Hawks' bench

and he started talking to the Hawks' coach. The Hawks' coach called time out and brought in this kid named Tommy Felton to pitch. He was supposed to be twelve, but he was about two times bigger than Godzilla. Somebody said he could throw a curve ball, but I wasn't sure. What I was sure about was that he could throw hard. You couldn't even see the ball, it was going so fast.

"This guy ought to be pitching for the Yankees," Mop said. "Nobody's going to get a hit off of him."

"He really looks good," Coach said.

Evans was supposed to be up, but Coach called him over and told Greg to get up.

"I can't get a hit off him," Greg said. He turned around on the bench so that he was facing away from Coach.

Coach went over to him and put her hand on his shoulder.

"Neither can anyone else," she said. "So you might as well try."

"No!" Greg said.

"Then we might as well start packing up," Coach said. "I'm not putting anybody else up."

"At least try," Jennifer said. "It won't kill you."

"You shut up."

"Start packing up," Coach said.

Greg made a sucking noise with his teeth. Then he got a bat and dragged it all the way to the plate.

The first ball that Tommy Felton pitched went right over the plate.

"Strike one!"

"Give it a ride, Greg!" Chrissie called out.

"He couldn't give it a ride if he had a token," Brian said.

"Strike two!"

Greg turned and gave the umpire a look.

"Come on, Greg," Coach called to him. "You can do it."

Tommy Felton was smiling. He pulled his hat down over his nose and leaned his head back. Then he took a deep breath, and started his windup.

Greg swung and the ball went up like a shot. At first their left fielder just stood there looking at it. Then he started back, but it didn't matter. That ball was gone! It went right over the fence and hit the truck that sells Cokes! It was a three-run homer.

We jumped all over Greg when he came home, and he had this big smile on his face. That was the first time I had ever seen him smile. Everybody was talking about that hit. It was just great. Even the Hawks were talking about it.

Coach shook Greg's hand and then she sat down again. She looked like she was tired. She was looking across the field and I looked to see what she was looking at. It was Mr. Treaster. He was talking to Tommy Felton and moving his hands low. I think he was telling Tommy he should have thrown the ball lower.

We were all kidding around and laughing when we packed things up. When we left, Greg was still hanging around the field. I think he wanted to think about that home run some more. I don't blame him.

"I didn't think Greg could hit that good," Moondance said. Me and him had to help Mop carry the equipment to her house. Now we were sitting around talking like you do when you win.

"I think he was watching us practice and got some ideas about how to hit," I said.

"He hits better than Brian," Mop said.

Mop had the coolest room you ever saw. Everything in the room was something other than it was supposed to be. The bed was shaped like a car. She had wallpaper that looked like a forest and the closet was like a cave. I think that was her father's idea. She even had a chest that looked like a pirate's chest.

"With Greg playing with us we'll probably win the championship again," Mop said. "We might even become legends."

"What's that mean?" Moondance had his feet on Mop's bed, but his body was hanging off and his head was on the floor.

"A legend is like Babe Ruth," Mop said. "Everybody knows about Babe Ruth. If we win the championship again, everybody might know about us. Then, a long time from now, when people come to the park they'll talk about us."

"What do you think they're going to say?" Moondance asked. When he was upside down his eyes didn't look like eyes. It looked like he had one eye in the middle of his forehead and he was talking out of it. It was just a little scary, but I didn't say anything.

"They'll say things like the greatest catcher in the world used to play right behind that home plate," Mop said. "Maybe they'll even put one of those brass stars on the ground or something."

"Get out of here!"

I didn't think they were going to put a star on the ground or anything like that. I did like the idea of little kids talking about us, and maybe growing up to want to be like us. I also thought about the French team. Mop had made arrangements to go down to the park and work with some of their guys.

After a while Coach came in and said she was going to the supermarket and asked if we wanted to come along and we all said no. I don't think she liked that very much. I don't know why grown-ups always ask you to say things like "yes" or "no" and then get mad if you say the wrong one.

"You sure?" Coach said. She put her hand on Mop's forehead.

"I'm sure," Mop said.

Coach smiled at Mop and Mop smiled at her, like they did sometime. It looked cool to see them do it.

Me, Mop, and Moondance headed down toward the park. Moondance was saying that maybe we should give Greg to the French team, but Mop was against it.

"Soon as this tournament is over and we start the regular season we're going to need him," she said.

"Then we can just get him back," Moondance said.

"Maybe," Mop said. "If Mr. Treaster and the Eagles don't get him first."

We went down to the park to see if we could find the French team. The park was full of kids. There were little kids and big kids and medium-size kids. Some kids from St. Al's were there in their brown-and-yellow uniforms and some kids from P.S. 117.

"You guys got a game today?" one of the kids I knew from P.S. 117 asked.

"We already played," I said. "We won."

The guys from the French team were kicking the baseball around. They were really good at that too. Stefan could keep it up in the air just by kicking it with the side of his foot. Mop said that the French guys were good with their feet because they played a lot of soccer. All of them, Stefan, Andre, and Claude, had their gloves on their heads.

"You two guys need fielding practice," Mop said, pointing at Stefan and Andre. "Get your gloves off your heads and get out there with T.J. and he'll show you what to do."

I went out in the field with Stefan and Andre and Mop hit a ground ball toward us.

"Catch it," I said.

Stefan missed it. He sort of almost caught it, but then I saw that he had his eyes closed.

"You have to keep your eyes open," I said.

"I can't do that," Stefan said. "When the ball comes the eyes close."

"No, you close them," I said.

"No, they close by themselves," he said.

"Mop, hit him another ball," I called to Mop. "Don't make it too hard."

This time I watched Stefan real close. The ball came bouncing right toward him. But just when it almost got to him he closed his eyes. He also turned his head away.

"You're closing your eyes," I said. "Watch how I do it.

"Mop! Hit it to me."

Mop hit a ball to me. It was harder than the one she hit to Stefan. I kept my eyes open all the way.

"You missed the ball," Stefan said.

"Yes, but I kept my eyes open, so I know where it went," I said.

But no matter what else Stefan did he kept closing his eyes. And then I had an idea.

"Okay, this time close your eyes and when the ball gets near you I'll tell you to open them," I said.

Stefan said okay. Then Mop hit the ball to him, but on the left side, and it went into the outfield. Andre went after it.

"Hit it right to him, Mop!" I said. "He's got his eyes closed!"

She gave me this funny look at first and then she hit it toward Stefan. It went right toward him.

"Get ready!" I said. I was just about to tell him to open his eyes when the ball kind of hopped up.

It hit him on the lip and he went staggering backward and then fell. By the time everyone got to him he was rolling around in the grass and yelling in French. Then Andre and Claude started talking French and they all started yelling and then Stefan got up and came over and pushed me.

"Why are you pushing me?" I asked.

Then Andre pushed me and Mop came over to see what was happening. When she came over Claude pushed her, and she knocked him down.

Stefan was crying and his lip was starting to swell. Moondance went and got the ball. Claude and Andre were looking at Stefan's face. I think he was hurt a little. I went and looked over Claude's shoulder. The lip was puffed up and he was really crying. Claude said something to me in French and they all left.

"What happened?" Mop asked.

"He kept closing his eyes when the ball came toward him," I said. "So I told him to keep his eyes closed until the ball got real near him and then open them up at the last minute."

"He didn't get them open in time?" she asked.

"Maybe I didn't tell him to open them soon enough," I said.

"How come Claude pushed me?" Mop asked.

"I don't know," I said.

"I think he was mad because somebody on his team got hurt," Moondance said.

"That happens when you play ball," Mop said. "You got to be able to take it."

Which was true. Sometimes you got hurt when you played ball, or you got hurt other times, and you just had to take it.

We thought for sure we had lost our friends on the French team. And that was too bad, because they seemed like nice guys.

The next day we had a speech from the mayor.

"So we are gathered here today in the spirit of friendship and cooperation." The mayor was standing in front of the stands. They had hooked up a microphone and some speakers so that you could hear him all over the park. He had been throwing a baseball around before and was sweating. Only, he sweated funny. He only sweated around his nose and under his arms.

"When are you going to bring down property taxes!" a tall man with a red face and a big mustache called out.

"This day is for the kids," the mayor said. "Don't try to take it away from them!"

"You're not going to have any kids in this city if you don't lower the taxes!" the man said.

The mayor shut off the microphone and started after the guy. I thought they were going to have a fight. I looked over at the other teams. The Japanese team was sitting very quietly. Half of the Mexican team was sitting and the other half was standing. I looked over at the French team and saw Stefan. He pointed at himself and then he pointed at me.

"Hey, Mop, look at Stefan," I said.

"What's he doing?" Mop asked.

"Beats me."

The mayor came back from arguing with the guy and started talking about how good it was that all the teams were getting along. Over at the French team Stefan was still giving us a look.

"You think he wants to fight me or something?" I asked Moondance.

"Who's going to fight?" Brian asked.

"Stefan has a fat lip and he thinks it's my fault," I said.

"Who's Stefan?" Brian asked.

"The kid from the French team," Mop said. "See that guy over there pointing to himself?"

"You know, if a French kid slaps you then you have to fight a duel," Brian said. "I saw that in a movie."

That was okay. I thought I could fight a duel. Maybe with swords. Somebody could drop a handkerchief and then we could sword fight. Sometimes Moondance and I played at sword fighting and I usually won. We only used sticks, but I figured it wouldn't be so different. It was better than fighting with your fists.

When the mayor finally stopped talking, which was after a long time, the teams just started walking around. Stefan and Claude came right over to us. Stefan had a funny look on his face and I thought for sure he wanted to fight a duel.

"You see my face?" Stefan said, pointing at his fat lip. "That happened because you are stupeed. But you are pretty much okay except for that."

"Don't you want to fight a duel?" Brian asked.

"Okay." Stefan shrugged. His smile was crooked because of his fat lip.

"I'm going to be the guy who gets his sword ready and stuff," Gregory said to Stefan. "And you're going to be dead."

"You guys are so stupeed I don't even know why you are okay," Stefan said. He walked away shaking his head.

"Don't worry about it," Greg said. Then he walked away.

"I think you're going to get killed," Brian said. "You see how Stefan said that he'd have a duel with you. He wasn't even worried."

"Greg wasn't worried either," I said.

"That's probably 'cause he's not going to be killed," Mop said.

Maybe Stefan was right, maybe we were a little stupeed.

Mom has this idea that all meals should have at least two or three different colors. So when we had spaghetti and meat sauce, which is white and red, we had to have something green too.

"Don't look at the broccoli that way," Mom said.

"I like broccoli," Moondance said.

"Suppose," I said, "that me and Moondance weren't really brothers. Like, I was really a prince or something. Then some guy kidnapped me and put me in a room with a thousand other kids and you couldn't tell which was the real me. The only way you could tell that I was really the prince was that I hated broccoli."

"Nobody hates broccoli," Dad said.

He didn't say anything else, just that nobody hated broccoli. That was wrong, because I hated broccoli. But Dad hated to be wrong. Anytime he was wrong he got mad. And if you told him he was wrong he got even madder.

Mom put some spaghetti on my plate and then put the meat sauce over it. "Maybe you're a prince, but you look enough like Moondance so that he must be a prince too."

"I'm the good prince," Moondance said. "The one who likes broccoli and spaghetti."

Which was true. Moondance liked everything. If you could eat it he liked it.

"And I think that if you had a thousand young people in a room you wouldn't be the only one who didn't like broccoli," Mom said.

"Mop doesn't like broccoli either," I said. "She said it's dinosaur food."

"Dinosaurs certainly grew to a good size," Mom said.

"And extinct," I said.

I wanted to talk more about broccoli. I didn't like to eat broccoli, but I liked to talk about it. But before you knew it we were in Family Discussion Time.

Once a week we have family discussion. That's when we could sit around and say anything we wanted for the first five minutes. After that was the time when Moondance talked a lot, Mom kept asking questions so that everybody talked some, and Dad got mad about something.

"How do you like the team this year?" Mom asked.

"It's okay," I said.

"We've got this new kid that's really good." Moondance had some spaghetti on his chin and pushed it up with his finger. "His name is Greg. He's kind of strange."

"He better than you?" Dad asked.

"I don't think that's important," Mom said.

A little muscle came up on Dad's jaw. It came twice while he looked like he was going to say something. Then he looked down at his spaghetti.

Mom noticed what Dad was doing and she got little frown marks near the corner of her mouth. That's how you can tell when they're not getting along sometimes. Dad gets little muscles in his jaw and Mom gets frown marks.

"Why's he strange?" Mom asked.

" 'Cause he doesn't want to talk to anybody else on the team and he gets mad so quick," Moondance said. "You just look at him and he's mad at you. And one time I saw him going into the woods, down near where that truck used to be."

There used to be an abandoned truck near the woods behind left field. Sometimes kids used to play in it and some of the parents made a petition and took it to city hall. Then somebody came and towed the truck away.

"Maybe that's a shortcut to his house," Mom said.

"No way," Moondance said. He was pushing his broccoli around in his spaghetti sauce. "That way doesn't lead anywhere."

"Every way leads to somewhere," Dad said. "You

just don't disappear. Where does this guy—what's his name?—live?"

"Greg," I said. "And I don't know where he lives, but I don't think every way leads to somewhere."

"Where you gonna go and not be somewhere?" Dad said.

"This is supposed to be family discussion," Mom said. "Not family argument."

"This is a discussion," Dad said.

"Suppose you go to outer space," I said. "Then there's nothing out there and you aren't anywhere."

"What?" Dad turned his head to one side. "What?"

"You could be way out and then you look around and there's nothing. No planets, no stars, no moon, no nothing."

Dad said something I couldn't understand, and then he said the universe was round. "So you go out for a while and then you turn around and start back because it's a circle," he said.

"What's on the other side of the circle?"

Dad looked at me, shook his head, and went back to his spaghetti. His little muscles were jumping around again. Mom started to ask him something, but he gave her a look and that was the end of family discussion. Dad isn't too good at family discussion.

We watched television for a while and nothing

bad happened. Moondance said that we hadn't gotten too much television yet, but I wasn't sure.

"Suppose we had hidden symptoms," I said. "Like when you have a cold or something and don't know it yet."

"We could get X-rayed," Moondance said. "Then maybe a television picture would show up on the X ray. Probably whatever program we watched too much."

"Or just interference."

"It could get into you and take you over like in *Invasion of the Body Snatchers*. And you wouldn't even know it because you would think you're imagining stuff and really the television programs would be going off in your head."

"Could be," I said. I lay down to see if I could figure out what I was thinking about. I didn't want to think about a television program, so I tried real hard to think about Mom and Dad. Mom and Dad always stayed up after we went to bed. Sometimes I think they never went to bed.

"Hey, T.J.?" Moondance called to me in a whisper.

"What?"

"How come we didn't talk about Mom having a baby?"

"You wanted to talk about it?"

"Yeah."

"How come you didn't?"

"I don't know," he said. "How come you didn't?"

"I didn't think about it," I said. "I guess I don't think about it too much."

"You don't want to think about it, or you just don't think about it?"

"I just don't think about it," I said.

"Good."

I also thought some more about Greg and I figured out that I didn't like it when another kid was mad all the time, and I didn't like it when a kid was sad all the time. One time Dad said that people didn't like it when other people weren't happy and they tried to shut them out of their mind. I was thinking about Greg, so he was still in my mind, but I was wishing that I didn't have to think about him, so I guess I'm just like everybody else.

"How come you said that maybe we weren't really brothers?" Moondance said when we were in our room alone.

"I didn't say we weren't really brothers," I said.

"Yes, you did," Moondance said. "You said that you could tell we weren't really brothers because you didn't like broccoli and I did."

"I was only making believe," I said.

"You shouldn't make believe about something like that," he said.

"When did you see Greg go into the woods?" I asked.

"Twice," Moondance said. "But I forget when."

* * *

Okay, the first thing that happened the next morning was that Mop called. That's the way Mop is. She'll get up extra early just so she can be the first person to call you in the morning. Once I woke up really early and called her first, but I didn't have anything to say and she got mad.

Anyway, she said we all had to go and meet Stefan and Claude in the park. I wasn't sure I wanted to, because they weren't really good at practice and I wasn't ready for a duel, but I said okay.

We got down to the park and Mop was there bouncing a ball off the side of the statue. I could see Stefan and he didn't have any swords, so I guess he forgot about the duel. Some Indian kids were playing cricket and when the ball came near me I threw it back to them.

The practice started off pretty good. Stefan and Claude didn't catch the ball too much, but they at least didn't get hit by it. We started talking about what was going to happen in the tournament. Stefan and Claude didn't even know about what a bunch of stinkers the Eagles were.

"Those guys beat you by a thousand runs!" Mop said.

"They only won one time, Moop," Claude said. "Next time we will win."

"To start with, it's not 'Moop,'" Mop said. "And

it doesn't matter how many times these guys play you, they are going to beat you."

"But I know why they win," Stefan said. "Because they play baseball better than we play baseball."

"That's not the point!" Mop said. She went over to the water cooler and put her thumb on the spigot, sending a stream toward the park benches.

"Is she mad at me?" Stefan asked.

"Yeah, I guess so," I said.

"Because we lost?"

Mop spun around. "You're not supposed to *like* losing!"

Then she turned around and looked across the field.

"And she is mad at the Eagles because they won us?" Stefan said.

Mop spun around again. "They didn't *won* you, they *beat* you, and you're not supposed to be so darn happy about it!" she said.

"Oh," Stefan said. Then he said something in French to Claude and Claude said "Oh" too. I didn't think they understood what Mop was being mad about.

I think what Mop was being mad about was that Claude and Stefan didn't know how to lose. When you lost you were supposed to be kind of sad and not too sad. When you won you were supposed to be happy but not too happy, so people would see that you were happy to win but you were unhappy because the other team lost. Or something.

e were going to have a practice game with Titi coaching us. Practice games were fun because you never lost.

"What're you making?" Mop looked down at Moondance's pile of dirt.

"It's a pyramid for ants," Moondance said.

"Your ants ever hear of Mopzilla?"

"What's that?" Moondance asked.

"This!" Mop banged her catcher's mask down on Moondance's pyramid.

Moondance grabbed Mop's mask and threw it into the tall grass. Mop smiled and went to get it.

Jennifer hit a foul ball that came over toward us and I caught it on the bounce and threw it back to Titi.

We watched as Chrissie pitched the ball up to Jennifer. Jennifer struck out and we had to go into the field.

Gregory got up and I figured he would get a hit off Mike. I didn't think he would hit a ball from our field to second base on the next field. I couldn't believe he could hit a ball so far. It took nearly five minutes just to go and get the ball. When I looked at the ball, one side of it, the side that said *Made in Haiti,* was flat. Really.

Evans was up next, and when he was batting I saw Titi talking to Greg. She pointed out to where he had hit the ball. I was just glad that Gregory was on our side.

Soon as we finished practice the ice cream truck came up and half the team went over to it. Titi said that the guys who went to the ice cream truck had to stay and pack up the gear. The rest of us could leave.

We started off the field. Mop was walking fast and me and Moondance were right behind her. Then we saw Greg. He was talking to a woman. She looked really raggedy and he was walking with her. It looked like they were in a big hurry. She stopped and turned toward him, but he didn't stop. He just kept going and left her there.

When we walked by her Moondance was between me and her, so I couldn't see her too good. She didn't look too good, maybe the kind of woman you see hanging around in the street a lot.

When we got home Moondance threw his glove into the corner the way he always did when he was mad. I knew what he wanted then. He wanted Mom to ask him what was wrong so that he could tell her that Mop stomped on his ant pyramid. But she fooled him. She didn't even talk to him.

"T.J." She said it with this real nice voice as she put her arm around my shoulder. "Go into the bathroom and wash up and then come back to the living room."

"You can't kill an ant by stepping on it," I told him. "People have been walking on the ground for a million years and there are still plenty of ants."

"She shouldn't have stepped on the pyramid," he said. "I'm helping the ants get revenge."

"Don't tell me about it," I said.

I wanted to figure out what the revenge of the ants was going to be. I like dreaming up ideas like that.

Sometimes things happen so fast, you don't even know they're going to happen. I didn't know I was going to throw a brussels sprout at Moondance. It just happened so fast—like *phht!* Moondance and I came to the table first. Dad was in the bathroom and Mom was serving. She put the brussels sprouts on our plates first and then went for the mashed potatoes, green and white. Moondance made a face at me and before I knew it the brussels sprout was flying across the table. Probably if I had known I was going to throw it I wouldn't have thrown it in the first place. Or at least I wouldn't have missed him. I probably would have thrown low enough to get the brussels sprout over the fish tank too.

Fish are Dad's hobby. Mom says he has thousands of dollars worth of stuff for the fish. The fish tank is only about one foot deep and the fish can swim that in no time. They can come up for air anytime they want to in about half a second, but Dad still got this machine that pumps air down to them. Anyway, he got mad when the brussels sprout went into the fish tank.

First he ran over and got it out and then he put it right on my plate and said I had to eat it. Then Mom got mad and said I didn't have to eat it and they started shouting and Dad told me and Moondance to go to bed and Mom said we didn't have to go until we had finished eating.

Then Dad said that as soon as we finished eating we had to go to bed and we couldn't watch television. Then Moondance said he didn't do anything and Mom said that was right and then she went on about how I had only made one little mistake.

"And you're sorry about that, aren't you, T.J.?" Mom asked.

"Yes, ma'am," I said.

"You know that brussels sprout could kill the fish?" Dad said. "Did you know that?"

"Then how come we have to eat it?" Moondance said.

Mom started laughing and Dad got up and went into the living room. He was really mad.

Mom said I still had to go to bed, but Moondance

didn't. What a bad day. First, I didn't get one hit at practice, then Dad got mad at me because he thought I was trying to hurt his stupid fish or something.

The next morning I heard the door slam and came out to find out what was going on.

"It's your father," Mom said. "I think he's still mad about the brussels sprout. I'm a little mad too. There are a lot of people around the world with very little to eat. It's very bad when some people, who have a lot to eat, waste food."

"Yes, ma'am." I knew she was right. She was good about that kind of thing. She was just as good as Titi, only Titi was a nun and it was her job to be good. Mom just did it because she didn't have anything else to do.

Anyway, Mom thought it would be a good idea to do something to make it up to Dad. We got another fishbowl from the closet and put some sand in it. Then we went out to the pet store. Mom liked shopping with us, even if it was just for a fish. We bought two neon tetras and put them in the bowl on top of the piano. Good place for them.

"Suppose he doesn't like them?" Moondance asked.

"Then we'll give it a brussels sprout and put it out of its misery," Mom said. "And don't you *dare* tell your father I said that."

We had a game with the French team that afternoon and Mom ironed our uniforms. I had put mine on and was just lacing up my sneakers when Mom started talking about there being more things in life than baseball.

"Like what?" Moondance asked. "What other kinds of things?"

I couldn't believe that Moondance said that. You *never* give a grown-up an excuse just to say anything they want.

"Things like music, and books, and art, and . . . and brussels sprouts," Mom said.

"And baseball . . ." I said.

Mom hit me on the head with the palm of her hand.

"What are we going to name the fish?" I asked.

"What would you like to name them?" she asked.

"How about T.J.?" I asked. "We could name them T.J. and T.J., Junior."

"How about naming one T.J. and one Moondance?" Mom said.

"I think we should name them both T.J. too," Moondance said. "They both look a little bit like him."

The Eagles crushed the Hawks! Evans saw the game and said that the Hawks couldn't do anything right. The pitcher for the Hawks walked the first three batters and hit the next two.

"Then the next three guys got hits!" Evans said. "The Eagles scored seven runs before the Hawks got anybody out!"

The way we started out against the French team, it looked like we were going to be just as bad as the Hawks. Titi was coaching and she had me playing third base instead of the outfield and had Mike playing first base. Bad news. The first three kids on the French team hit ground balls, and when our team threw to first base, Mike missed the ball three times in a row. That was bad.

Then the French team started cheering like crazy in the dugout because they were ahead and Brian got mad. Brian was pitching. He walked the next three guys and Titi had to go out and talk to him.

"Okay, we need a triple play or something," Mike said.

We all said that we could still win the game. We just had to buckle down and be ready.

"Yeah, and maybe catch a few balls at first base," Brian said, giving Mike a dirty look.

I looked over at Mop. Usually she said something when Brian started complaining. This time she didn't. She didn't even put her catcher's mask on the top of her head the way she usually did. I couldn't see if she was crying or not.

I was just hoping that one of the French kids would hit the ball to me. I would grab it and tag third for one out. Then I would throw it to Moondance at second for the second out. Then he would throw it to Mike at first for the triple play!

It was funny, I was just hitting my glove and thinking about that triple play when the big kid on the French team, the one who was the catcher, hit the ball right at me. It was a hard grounder, maybe the hardest grounder ever hit in Lincoln Park. I grabbed that ball so fast it wasn't even funny. It hurt like crazy, but that didn't stop me. I started to throw to second base but then I forgot I hadn't tagged third base yet. So I started toward third, but then the runner was coming toward third and I tagged him. I didn't exactly tag him, because I missed him by maybe just one inch. Then I ran to the bag.

"Safe!" the umpire yelled.

When I say he yelled, I mean he really yelled. He

scared me and I dropped the ball. But only for like half a second at the most, not even that. I picked it up and threw it to Moondance. I didn't want to throw it over his head, so I threw it a little low. It bounced a few times but it went right to second base.

"Safe!" the umpire said.

Then Moondance threw the ball to Mike at first. But by that time the batter was already standing there.

"Safe!" the first-base umpire called out.

We had just missed our first triple play.

Brian threw his glove down and kicked it. You don't do that in our league, and the umpire threw him out of the game. I never saw a guy so mad before. Baseball didn't agree with him too much.

"You stink!" he said as he went past me.

Then I understood what his problem was. He didn't understand the game. I almost had a triple play—*a triple play*—and he was mad. You couldn't get any better than a triple play, because there were only three outs to an inning.

The game got down to the last inning and we were losing seventeen to fifteen. Titi had put in Chrissie and she was up. She hit the first ball on the ground toward third base. The kid on third base started to get the ball when the shortstop came over and got it right in front of him. Then he threw it over their first baseman's head and Chrissie was on base.

Their third baseman and their shortstop got into an argument in French. An argument in French is pretty cool because it didn't seem so much like an argument. You could tell it was an argument though, because the third-base guy kept sticking out his tongue at the shortstop.

Okay, Joey was up next. He hit a ground ball to their shortstop. This time the third-base guy ran over and got the ball right in front of the shortstop. He threw the ball to second base, but the second baseman wasn't on second base. He was just sort of standing between first and second, watching the game.

When the ball went into right field Chrissie ran to third base and Joey ran to second.

Titi called us over.

"Okay, we're only two runs behind now," she said. "If we make contact with the ball we'll be all right. Don't try to hit home runs. Singles will win it for us."

Everybody said okay. And then Moondance struck out and Jennifer got up.

She never even swung the bat. Their pitcher threw the ball three times and the umpire called three strikes. We were down to our last out.

Evans was up. Evans strikes out more than anybody in the whole world except maybe Benny, but he's really little. I thought we had lost for sure, but that's when the fight started.

Evans swung on the first pitch and hit a ground ball to third base. The third baseman started yelling at the shortstop. He was holding up his hand to keep him away from the ball because it was really the third baseman's ball. It really was, only he didn't catch it. It went right under his glove.

Then he started yelling at the shortstop and the shortstop came over and yelled back at him. All of this was in French, so I didn't know what they were saying, but I knew they were pretty mad. Then they were wrestling around on the field and the shortstop was hitting the third-base guy with his glove. Chrissie and Joey came in to score.

The umpire went over to the French coach and talked to him and pointed at the kids. The French coach kept nodding his head and then he went over and yelled at his guys. That seemed to calm them down a little.

The score was tied and Greg got up. The umpire called strike one and Greg backed out and gave him a look. Then he moved up to the plate and hit the next ball about two and a half miles. It went between their left fielder and center fielder. I knew it was going to be a home run and it was.

We all cheered and banged Greg on his back. We started to pack up our gear as the French team started fighting again.

Their coach was mad and he was yelling in French and pretty soon their whole team was yelling in French. I wish I knew some French because I wanted to yell something too. Anyway, I yelled "Murdeeer!" because that's what it sounded like some of them were saying.

While we were packing I saw the woman that I had seen Greg talking to before. He saw her at the same time I did and started walking away. He was walking fast too. He didn't walk toward her, he just walked away from us toward the path that led out of the park. And when I turned back toward the woman she was walking away too.

When we got home Moondance started watching television. He says he hates television, but he always watches it. I went into the kitchen and watched Mom cooking. I know she likes me to watch her cooking, because she starts acting like the people who cook on television.

There were some things I wanted to talk to her about, but I wasn't sure how to get it going.

Sometimes I talk too much. I don't *always* talk too much, because that's not what I'm really like. Mostly I'm really like the strong, silent type. That's probably why I talk too much sometimes, because I save up too many things to say when I'm not talking. But sometimes I say just the right thing. That's when my perfect side shows up.

I've got two sides, like everybody. A side that is

just about okay and a side that is perfect. When I make mistakes, drop a glass and break it, something like that, then that's the side that is just okay. It's not terrible, because anybody can make a mistake.

But then sometimes my perfect side comes out and I know just the right thing to say and everything.

Mom has cookbooks that tell her how to make any kind of food. She had her German cookbook opened up. She said she was making kadiffle houses, something like that. Anyway, that's like making potato mudpies. You mash up some potatoes and mix them with flour and you make those kadiffle houses.

"You know what else you can make with flour and water?" I asked.

"What else?" Mom asked.

"Paste."

Mom gave me this funny look, then went back to mixing up the potatoes and flour and stuff. "You saying this looks like paste to you, young man?" she asked.

It was her smiling voice, so I know she wasn't mad.

"No," I said. "Only, that's how you make paste. With flour and water. So you got paste and potatoes."

"That's not nice to say," she said. "This is going to be delicious. It's a German dish."

"Can I ask you a question?"

"Sure."

"A drop of sweat just fell in the bowl," I said.

"You're not supposed to notice that," she said, wiping the side of her face on her shoulder. "What did you want to ask me?"

"Do you think of the baby much?"

"Sometimes," she said.

"What do you think about?" I asked.

"Same things I used to think when we were thinking of adopting a child," she said. "What he's going to look like. What he's going to be like, that kind of thing."

"It's going to be a boy?"

"The doctor thinks so."

"Oh."

"Is it better getting a surprise or going out and finding a kid that looks just like you want?" I asked.

"I like going shopping for what I want," Mom said.

"T.J. notices things," Dad said.

"Like what?" Mom asked.

"Little things," Dad said. He was making an origami frog. That's what he said he was doing, but he had been working on it for about an hour. "He noticed that the picture in the living room was crooked."

"That's right, he did," Mom said.

"You see little things like that," Dad said, unfolding the frog again, "you can go a long way. It's a gift."

I didn't think too much of noticing things at first. But when I thought about it a little I noticed that I did notice a lot of things. I did notice that the picture was crooked, like Dad said. I also noticed two more things.

The first thing I noticed was that Greg was not only a different kind of guy, he also liked to fight a lot. He told me he thought I could kill Stefan in a duel, but then when Stefan didn't say any more about it, Greg acted like he really didn't care.

Sometimes he acted like he really didn't care about anything and then all of a sudden you said something that you thought he didn't care about and *pow!* you're right in the middle of a fight with him.

He got into a fight with a kid in Lincoln Park. Boo Addison told me, and Boo never lies, that Greg started the fight. He said this kid didn't do anything to Greg. They were fooling around and the kid threw some dirt on him and he got mad.

Boo said Greg didn't say anything. He just started punching the guy like crazy. Two men came over and stopped the fight and told them to shake hands, but Greg wouldn't do it. Boo said he didn't know why Greg hit the guy. I don't know why Greg does things like that. I figured maybe I would talk to him and figure him out.

The other thing I noticed is that no matter what goes on, everything else goes on too. You figure if something important was happening everything else would stop and wait until it was over. Say the World Series was going on. Well, other things keep going on like there was no World Series. You still have to go to school, you still have to eat breakfast and do homework. Everything.

Greg was being different. I was being sad. And everything else was still going on.

The Eagles played the Nagasaki Knights and lost by one run. What happened was this. The Eagles were up in the top of the sixth inning. Chris Baber was on first and Rocky was up with one out. Rocky hit a long fly ball and took off running. It was the highest ball I had ever seen in my entire life. The ball went to the outfield and the Japanese outfielder almost got to it and then he tripped and the ball got past him.

Then the umpire called Rocky out. Then everybody was calling the umpire crazy and yelling because the ball was still in the outfield.

"You passed the runner on first," the umpire yelled. "You're automatically out!"

Meanwhile, Chris and Rocky from the Eagles are standing at third base. Then Rocky gives Chris a push and tells him to run home. Only, he pushed him too hard and he fell down. By that time the Knights had the ball. Rocky was standing on third base and so Chris started for home and got tagged out.

Mr. Treaster was so mad I thought he was going to explode. He yelled at the umpire. Then he yelled at Chris Baber, then he yelled at Rocky. It didn't make any difference, the Eagles had lost.

The way I figured it was that if the Knights beat the Eagles, they had a pretty good chance of beating us again.

"We have to use some psychology on them," Jennifer said.

"What do you know about psychology?" Brian said. "You can't even spell it."

"You wouldn't even know if I spelled it right or not," Jennifer said.

"I don't think psychology is going to help against them," Coach said. "They're a very good team. We will have an extra practice before we play, though."

We had a practice. No, we had a terrible practice. Nobody caught anything. Nobody hit the ball either. We were just so bad it wasn't even funny.

"Maybe we got it out of our system," Benny said.

"What's that mean?" I asked.

"Sometimes, if you're going to do something wrong you're just going to do it anyway," he said. "You might as well get it over with. So if you don't do well at practice you might do okay at a real game."

That made sense.

We were pretty hopeful until Greg and Joey DeLea didn't show up for the game. Joey's mother called Coach and said that he had an upset stomach, but we didn't know where Greg was.

Moondance was pitching. He was pitching okay, but not as fast as he pitched last year. The Japanese guys scored two runs in the first inning. When we got up we didn't even get a hit.

Then in the second inning their first man up got a triple. He was a pretty big guy. Mop called time out and went out to the mound. She called me and Mike over.

"I'm going to pick this guy off third base," she

said. "You keep talking to him and then when he comes off the base I'll get him."

"Suppose he doesn't come off the base?" I asked.

"Tell him to go off," Mop said.

She turned and went back behind the plate. I knew what I was supposed to do. I was going to use psychology to get the Japanese guy out.

"What's your name?" I asked him.

He didn't answer.

"You can't talk English?"

"I can talk English," he said.

"Say something in English," I said.

"I just did."

"So what's your name?"

"Yoshiro," he said.

"Strike one!" the umpire called out.

The Japanese guy, Yoshiro, gave me a look and then he smiled at me.

You can't take a lead until the ball crosses the plate. As soon as the ball got to the plate on the next pitch Yoshiro ran about three steps. Mop threw the ball down to me. Only, she threw it too close to Yoshiro. It almost hit him. I thought it was going to hit him, so I moved over to get the ball when it bounced off him. Only, it didn't hit him and it went past him and went down the line. Then he got up and ran home.

Mop got mad at me because she thought I should have caught the ball.

"If you hadn't thrown the ball he would still be on third base," I told her.

That shut her up good. She just went back to catching, shaking her head.

The score was pretty close up until the last inning. We were losing, three to two. I figured we might lose by one run the way that the Eagles had lost.

Mop got up first. She wasn't even speaking to me. I think she was just mad at everybody. The Knights' pitcher threw the ball and Mop hit a line drive down the right-field line and Mop wound up on second base. Then Brian walked. Chrissie got up and struck out. So did Moondance, which made two outs. But Jennifer got a hit and the bases were loaded!

Up comes Mike, and Coach calls him over. I was on deck, so I heard them talking.

"Their third baseman is playing way back," Coach said. "Try bunting down the third-base line."

Mike nodded and I looked at their third baseman. It was Yoshiro. He looked at me and then at their pitcher.

Their pitcher wound up, and just as he started to throw the ball Yoshiro moved in real close. Mike swung at the ball and hit it right past him.

"Way to go, Mike!" Coach yelled.

The ball went to the outfield and Mop and Brian came in to score. We won!

"I told Mike to bunt," Coach said to Mop when she came over. "But when he saw their third baseman come in, he used his head and swung away."

Everybody was jumping up and down and Titi was trying to get them calmed down. I looked for Mop and saw her putting her stuff in the game bag. Mr. Treaster was over by the gate. His mouth was shut real tight and his ears were red. He was ticked off because we had beat the Knights.

Stefan had been watching the game and he came over to us as we started off the field.

"He looks like he's going to blow a gasket," Mop said.

"What's a gasket?" I asked her.

"It's what a car has and it blows up when it gets too hot," Mop said.

I wondered how come Mop knew more than me and we go to the same school.

"Hey, Mop, how come you know more than me and we go to the same school?"

"Because girls are smarter than boys, so we know more," Mop said. "Everybody knows that."

"I don't think that's true," Stefan said.

"Of course it's true," Mop said. "But you don't know it because you're boys."

Stefan gave me a look and shook his head "no," but he didn't let Mop see him doing it.

* * *

The next time we had practice Mop told Stefan to come by so that he could learn something. We were all sitting around waiting for practice to begin when Mop started talking about how we had to win the tournament.

"How come?" I asked.

"Because my dad said people expected us to win," Mop said. She was lying on her back with her feet against the bench. Moondance was sitting on the fence and Chrissie Testor was sitting with me on the bench. "He said when people see the champions lose, then they think the whole country is falling apart. So if we just go on and win the tournament, we can go to Japan and the whole country can just be cool again."

"Taiwan always wins the Little League tournaments," Chrissie said.

"That's because the teams they're playing against aren't the champions, they just trying to be the champions," Mop said. "But we *are* the champions, right?"

"I guess so."

"Then we gotta win," Mop said.

"I don't think Coach wants to win that badly," Chrissie said. "You hear what she said about it's only a game and everything? You ask me, she's more interested in getting some goodwill or something like that going."

"Well, that's not the way I am," Mop said.

I looked over at Mop to see if she was smiling or anything, but she wasn't. "Who do we have to play next?" I asked.

"The Mexican team," Jennifer said. "And if we don't stop dropping the ball at third base, we're going to lose by fifty runs."

"Don't worry," I said. "I'm playing third base."

"That's what I'm worried about," Jennifer said.

"Where's that creep, Greg?" Chrissie asked.

"Who cares?" Jennifer said.

"He's good," Mop said. "We need him. We'll have to go find him. Anybody know where he lives?"

Nobody knew. Titi came over and said it was time to practice.

I had an idea, but I didn't say it. What I thought we should do was to miss the ball in practice like Benny said. Then we could get it out of our system. We had a bad practice before the game against the Japanese team and we had won that game. Maybe it would work again.

I didn't say it or anything, but I still had a bad practice. I missed almost every ball that came to me, and I knew I had it made for the game.

When we finished practicing the French team came onto the field. A guy from the *Jersey Journal* showed up at the game and started taking pictures.

"Take my picture!" Evans started yelling.

But this guy took pictures mostly of the French

team. Then he took some pictures of some Japanese guys and some Filipino guys who weren't even playing on a team. They were just playing basketball in the park. The last thing he took pictures of was Mr. Treaster and Coach.

"Hey, how come you took pictures with Mr. Treaster?" Brian asked.

"Because the photographer asked us," Coach said.

"It probably hurt his face to ask him to take your picture," Titi said. "That's his friend from the *Journal*."

"Maybe he's turning over a new leaf," Coach said. "I wonder." Coach rubbed her nose with the palm of her hand, the way she does sometimes. "I wonder."

I got to talk to Greg. Bad move. My mom and I went down to the Hudson Mall to do some shopping. When I saw Greg outside the store I told Mom I was going to hang out with him until she finished shopping, and she said okay.

"If Greg leaves, come in and find me," she said. "I'll probably be in fresh vegetables."

It was funny thinking about Mom in fresh vegetables. I imagined her sitting on the shelf surrounded by carrots and tomatoes. It was a funny picture.

"How come you didn't show up for the game yesterday?" I said when I found Greg sitting on the fence outside the supermarket.

"How come you ask so many questions?" he said.

"Because I wanted to know how come you didn't show up," I said.

"You lose?" he asked.

"We won," I said. "Coach was going to call your house, but she didn't have your telephone number."

"I don't want nobody calling me," he said.

"Then you have to be on time," I said. "Why don't you tell your mother when the game is going to be and she can tell you when to go?"

"Why don't you get out of my face, man!"

Greg came right up to me and pushed his face against mine. I pushed him away and he swung at me. He hit me right in the face. He looked at me for a minute and then he turned and ran away.

He didn't hurt me. Mostly he surprised me, because I didn't know why he hit me. But then I remembered something. I saw him headed toward the road that went in front of the mall and I ran after him. He turned and saw me coming and stopped. When I got to him he had his feet spread apart and his fists up.

"Come on, sucker!" he said, winding up his right fist. "I got something for you!"

"I just came to tell you we're on this team together," I told him. "We're on the same side."

"Why you going away?" he called after me when I started back toward the supermarket. "You scared?"

I wasn't scared when I left him, just kind of excited and maybe nervous. But by the time I got back to the supermarket I was a little scared, or maybe just more nervous.

Greg had hit me in the face for nothing. Sometimes, before Moondance and me got adopted and we were at the Academy, kids would start fights and the nuns used to break them up and ask us how come we were fighting when we were all in the same place and doing the same thing.

"We're all in this together," they used to say.

I started to go into the supermarket, but changed my mind and sat outside awhile. Sometimes, back at the Academy, the kids would settle their own problems. Sometimes we didn't really settle anything, just sort of let things cool out because we knew how each other felt. Knowing how Greg felt might be harder, but I was going to try.

When I went inside I found Mom in frozen foods. She asked me if I wanted french fries. I gave her a hug and she put the french fries in the shopping basket.

Mop called me in the morning. "My mom's *furious*," she said. "And so am I."

"About what?"

"I'm too *furious* even to mention it," she said. "Go find the *Journal* and turn to page twenty-four!"

Moondance and I went out and bought the paper. On the front page there was a story about somebody dumping something illegal on the mayor's front lawn. I knew that didn't make Mop mad, so I turned to the sports pages. Right there, on page twenty-four like she said, was a picture of Coach and Mr. Treaster. Under the picture there was a story.

American Coaches Team Up to Stop Alien Invasion
"It's a matter of national pride," said Eagles Coach Irwin Treaster. "We represent America in an American game. I'm sure all the local coaches agree."

We called Mop back.

"You got the newspaper in your hand?" I asked her.

"Right in front of me!" she said.

It was funny looking at the same newspaper she was looking at and at the same time and everything.

"Ask her, is Coach mad," Moondance said.

"Is she *mad*?" Mop had heard Moondance. "She's so mad she's hopping around like a frog on a frying pan and I'm even madder! You guys meet me down at the ballpark right away!"

We told Mom what had happened and that we

had to meet Mop down at the ballpark. Mom said that maybe we shouldn't talk too much about what was in the newspapers until after some of the parents had talked about it. We said okay, but we knew Mop was going to talk about it.

"Why is everybody so mad?" Moondance asked when we got to the park.

"Are you against the Japanese team?" Mop squinched her eyes up. "Are you? Well, *are* you?"

"Yeah," Moondance answered.

"Why?" Mop asked. Her nose was maybe one inch away from my brother's.

"Because when they play they want to beat us and we want to beat them," Moondance said.

"Don't be stupid," Mop said. "I know you're against them in baseball, but are you against them because they're the Japanese team?"

"I don't know," Moondance said, looking over at me.

"Well, you ought to know," Mop said. "Because that Mr. Treaster is trying to make it look like we don't like the Japanese guys or something. That's why my mom is mad."

A bee landed right on the edge of Moondance's cap and Mop took a swipe at it. It just flew up in the air and came down on his cap again.

"So what's Coach going to do?" I asked.

"I think she should punch him out," Mop said. She hit Moondance's cap and knocked it off. The bee buzzed around between us and we all backed off in a big hurry.

"You want to go down to the playing fields?" I asked.

"No, we got to make some plans," Mop said. "Your mom tell you about the picnic?"

"What picnic?"

Moondance had taken off his hat and started swinging at the bee. Every time he swung he missed, but the bee stayed near him.

"Stop swinging your stupid hat," Mop said. "You're just confusing the bee."

Moondance stopped swinging and sure enough the bee stopped buzzing around and landed right on Mop's shoulder.

"*Eeoooow!*" She hit at the bee and knocked it off, and we all took off toward the water fountain.

"That bee stung you?" I said when reached the water fountain.

"No, I was yelling just in case he did," Mop said.

We looked each other over to make sure the bee hadn't followed us.

"That stupid bee thought I was a flower," Moondance said.

"Hey, look at that," Mop said.

We looked to see where Mop was looking. It was Gregory. He was walking with the same woman I had seen him with before.

"You want to go over and say something to him?" Mop asked.

"I don't think so," I said, thinking about the last time I had tried to talk to him. "Let's just see where they go."

"You want to go and see if there's a game going on over the bridge?" Moondance asked.

"No," I said. I was still watching Gregory and the woman. The way he walked next to her I could tell it was his mom.

"They don't look like they're doing too good," Mop said, nodding toward Greg and the woman.

Mop was right. Greg and the woman didn't look as if they were doing well. She was wearing a long blue dress and I knew I had seen it and her before. Sometimes she used to sit in a little park near Duncan Avenue.

"Don't stare at them," I said, looking away.

"You think that's Greg's mother?" Moondance asked.

"C'mon, let's keep walking," I said.

"Yeah," Mop answered him.

I turned back and saw them go down a small road near where the old bridge used to be. Nobody ever went there anymore.

"So what about the picnic?" Moondance went on.

"Oh, yeah." Mop looked back toward Moondance. "There's going to be this picnic near the fountain on Saturday morning. We're going to invite all the teams over and be intercultural and everything."

"What does that mean?" Moondance asked.

"Intercultural means that you figure out how somebody's different and let them know that you know it and don't mind too much."

"It doesn't sound like much fun," I said.

"Yeah, but if that's what my mom wants," Mom said, "that's what my mom gets."

We walked around the park some more and Mop talked about how she would knock Mr. Treaster out if he said anything to her.

"I'd kick his ankle," she said. "Then when he bent over to grab it—*pow!*"

We didn't see Mr. Treaster until the next day. He was smiling and walking around like he had won a prize or something. Coach went over to talk to him and he just turned and walked away. There were some guys with cameras that turned out to be from another newspaper and they wanted to talk to Coach. They came over to where we were doing our stretching exercises. At first Coach wouldn't talk to them, but then she looked at us, and she did. I think she wanted us to listen. Anyway, we all did.

"So what's wrong with an American team winning the tournament?" a guy with a skinny face asked.

"There's nothing wrong with an American team

winning the tournament," Coach said. "But what we're supposed to be doing is having a nice time and meeting young athletes from other countries. Winning isn't everything."

"Then how come when the teams from other countries play in the Little League they always win?" the guy said. "They don't send just any team over here. They send their best."

"Trying to win a game and making winning the only thing that you're interested in are two different things," Coach said.

"So you don't care if the Elks win this thing?" the newspaper guy asked.

"We care," Coach said, her neck turning red, "and we will try to win!"

"You see yourself as some kind of crusader or something?" the newspaper guy asked.

"No," Coach said. "But when you see something you think might be wrong, it's not enough just to look at it. You have to take a stand."

"Sounds like a crusade to me." The newspaper guy was smiling like he had done something great, and Coach was mad and Mop was mad and I was kind of mad too. In fact, I was really mad. I wanted to win just so that the Eagles wouldn't win.

We watched the Mexican team work out a little more and then Mop said that we should go get a soda.

"No, I got something else to do," I said.

I thought Moondance would stay with me, but he walked Mop home.

Coach was still there, talking to Titi. I went over and asked her for Greg's address. She had all the addresses in the back of the book where she kept the team records. She looked up Greg's address and gave it to me.

"We still don't have a telephone number for him," she said.

The address I got for Greg was 223 Grant Avenue. Grant Avenue was in a kind of a tough neighborhood. It made me a little nervous to go there, but I went anyway. I found Grant Avenue pretty easy, but I couldn't find the number 223. I saw Bob, our postman, and asked him.

"There is no 223," Bob said. "That used to be a drugstore, but it closed years ago."

If a kid gave a false address like that, I figured he had to be on the Most Wanted list or have some pretty serious problems. I had the feeling that Greg had some big problems.

Saturday was the day we were supposed to have the picnic. The day was cloudy and dark.

"I hope it rains," Moondance said.

"How come?" I asked.

"We have to go to the picnic," Moondance said. "If it rains they might call it off."

Two guys from each of the American teams had to come early and help set things up. And guess who got picked from the Elks? Right, me and Moondance.

"What kind of a picnic is this going to be?" I asked. It sure didn't look good with balloons all over the place. They were on the bushes, on the fence, and tied to just about everything.

"It's going to be a drippy picnic," Mop said. "And if you say one thing about how I'm dressed, I'm going to split your lip in about six places."

"You look okay," I said.

"You think I can't split your lip?" Mop said, pushing up the sleeve on her blouse.

"I said you look okay," I said.

"Not now, stupid," Mop said.

"Hi, guys." Coach came over carrying a big pan of hot dogs. "Mop, go change."

Mop gave us a look and then went into the ladies' room.

"You guys can get the paper plates from the car and put them on the table," Coach said.

That was pretty easy and we went over to the car and got them. I didn't know why they needed any of the guys from the team, because every mother in the whole world was there.

We got the paper plates and put them out and then we mostly stood around until Mop came back.

"She's got her fighting clothes on," Moondance said.

I looked over and saw that what Moondance said was true. Mop had on a dress. When she has a dress on you can't say anything bad to her because she'll hit you so fast you won't know what happened. And Mop can really hit hard. That's because girls have more bones in their hands than boys.

The Mexican team was the first to show up. Everybody shook their hands and started giving them food and everything and they seemed happy. Then the Japanese team showed up. Before you knew it the whole place was jammed full of people.

The guy who brought the food from the restaurant is named Tee-Bo. That's probably not his real name, but that's what everybody calls him. Sometimes my mom goes to his restaurant and most of the people we know in the neighborhood get food from his place. Anyway, he kept bringing in all these pans full of fried chicken and spareribs and potato salad and that kind of stuff. The hot dogs were already there and some of the other parents had brought cakes and sodas. We had so much food we could have opened our own restaurant. The picnic got kind of interesting because a lot of the grown-ups were eating everything in sight and telling us what to eat and not to eat.

"We should have thought more about the menu," Coach was saying.

"I think it's pretty good," Moondance said, stuffing some cake into his mouth.

"That's what I'm afraid of," Coach said.

We were playing Pin the Tail on the Donkey when the French guys showed up. You know who could play Pin the Tail on the Donkey great? This Mexican kid. You could turn him around thirty-five times and he'd find the donkey. He was so good even the other Mexican kids didn't believe him. One of them put his hand right in front of his face and he didn't move or anything. He just went right to the donkey and pinned the tail pretty close to where it was supposed to be.

One of the Mexican kids said he was faster than Brian and they almost got into a fight, but my grandma, who had helped serve, stopped them.

"Now, if you children want to race, you line up right here," she said, pointing to a line on the ground, "and you start when I start. The first one that reaches the fence, wins."

Grandma Lois pushed her toe against the line and Brian and the Mexican kid, I think his name was Paco, lined up next to her.

"You boys ready?" Grandma Lois asked.

Brian was on one side of her and Paco was on the other side. They looked around her at each other and Brian gave Paco a mean look.

"Get set!" Grandma Lois leaned over the line.

When Paco saw Brian clenching his fists, he clenched his too.

"Go!"

Grandma Lois took off first. Brian was a little surprised to see her go and Paco started off before him. Then Brian put his head down and ran with all his might. Everybody started yelling for whoever they wanted to win. Paco caught Grandma Lois just before the finish line and Brian came in last.

You know how mad Brian was? He was so mad he walked right over to a tree and started crying. That's pretty mad.

Mom went over to Grandma Lois and she had this look on her face like she was as surprised as I was that Grandma Lois was so fast. Paco was fast too. Maybe not as fast as Greg, but fast. I looked around for Greg, but I didn't see him.

Mr. Treaster and some of the Eagles showed up late but you could tell they weren't going to have a good time. Mr. Treaster stood near the fence with his arms folded and Rocky and Chris Baber stayed close to him. He couldn't mess the picnic up, though. Everybody was having too good a time even to notice him.

Jennifer had an idea for a new game. You picked a partner and then you threw popcorn to each other and whoever caught the most popcorn in their mouth in two minutes won the contest.

"I'll pick the teams," Coach said.

Me and a Mexican kid named Jorge were one team, a French kid and the Mexican coach were on another team, and Mop and a Japanese kid were on the last team. Jennifer, the Japanese coach, and a woman from the nearby bodega were the official counters.

Me and Jorge were up first. He threw one and then I threw one and we both missed. Then he started laughing and I started laughing and it took a while before we started again. This time we both caught a popcorn. Then he threw his and I caught it, but when I threw mine he missed. We ended up with his catching four and me catching six for a total of ten.

Then the French kid threw his and the Mexican coach caught it, but the French kid missed. The Mexican coach couldn't throw that well. Some of the time his popcorn went right over the French kid's head. They caught nine pieces of popcorn.

Then Mop and the Japanese kid, Akiro, started. Mop caught hers and Akiro caught his. Then Mop caught another one and Akiro caught another one. But Mop was really slow when she threw and Akiro wanted her to hurry up.

"Throw faster!" he said.

"I'm a catcher, don't tell me how to throw!" Mop said.

They had six after the first minute and then Mop missed two in a row.

"Throw faster!" Akiro said, looking at the clock we were using to time the contest.

Mop was getting a little mad and she threw one too low. Then Akiro threw one too high. Before you knew it they only had fifteen seconds left.

"What's the score?" Mop asked.

"You need three more to win," Jennifer said.

"Quick, open your mouth!" Mop yelled. "Wider!"

Mop grabbed two handfuls of popcorn and threw them at Akiro. The popcorn hit him in the mouth, bounced off his head, fell off his chest and went down his shirt. Everybody was laughing and yelling.

"She won! She won!" Jennifer said.

"No, she didn't," Coach said. "She was supposed

to throw one at a time and take turns. T.J. and Jorge won."

We played some more games and they were pretty good. They were the kind of games that everybody had fun playing and watching. Then we ate some more and finally Coach said that we should calm down for a few minutes before the picnic was over. That picnic lasted for two hours and it was the best picnic I've ever been to.

When it was time to leave everybody was still laughing. I looked around for Mr. Treaster and he was standing with Rocky looking mean, and Chris Babar was wrapping a piece of cake in a napkin to take with him. Coach was wiping up soda somebody had spilled on the table and Mop and Jennifer were saying good-bye to everybody. I was looking at them because Jennifer was kissing everybody on both cheeks like they do in the movies, which was cool. That's why I saw Akiro come up. He had a plate of ice cream when he got near the door. He was saying something to Mop and then started pointing his finger at her. Then she started pointing her finger at him and it was her finger that knocked the paper plate out of his hand and sent the ice cream flying onto his shirt.

"You have embarrassed me and made me look foolish," Akiro was saying when I got over to them. "If you were not a girl I would crush you like a twig."

"You just want to try it? You just want to try it?" Mop pushed her sleeves up to her elbow and her nose right into Akiro's face.

He pushed her away and she went down pretty hard.

"I am a sumo wrestler!" he said. "And sumo wrestlers don't fight girls!"

"I got a boyfriend named Four Times Seven!" Mop said.

We all stopped and looked at Mop. I couldn't help smiling. Mop was smiling too. Akiro looked at each of us.

"Is he much bigger than me?" he asked Mop.

"No." Mop was on her feet. "He's a lot smaller than you, but he'll take care of any stupid sumo wrestler!"

"Well, where is he?" Akiro said.

"Just be at home plate Monday morning at ten o'clock," Mop said. "If you have the nerve."

"I don't think we should get into a fight with the Japanese kids," Moondance said as we left the park.

"We're not going to get into a fight with them," Mop said. "We're going to get Four Times Seven!" Four Times Seven was a cat, and the roughest cat anybody had ever even heard about. It was supposed to be a pussycat, but it was big enough to be a wildcat. But I knew what Moondance meant.

"Coach was talking about us getting along with the other teams," I said. "That's what Moondance means."

"Do American kids fight?" Mop stopped and looked at me with her head tilted to one side.

"Yeah."

"That's what we do sometimes, but it doesn't mean we don't get along, right?"

"Sort of."

"See?"

We saw Jennifer's mother on West Side Avenue

and Mop decided to go to Jennifer's house, so me and Moondance said good-bye and started home.

"Do you know what she meant when she said 'See?' " Moondance asked.

"Nope."

"Then how come you didn't say anything?"

"How come you didn't say anything?"

" 'Cause I thought you knew what she meant," Moondance said.

"And I thought you knew what she meant," I said.

"Mom said that sometimes when somebody wants to do something they either figure out a way to make it seem all right or they don't think about it too much," Moondance said. "That's what I think Mop was doing."

"Mom said that to you?"

"Yep."

Mom never said things like that to me. She probably figured that I usually knew most things, so she didn't have to say them to me. Which is more or less true.

"What's the *matter* with you guys!" Brian was yelling at everybody. "Come on and play ball!"

Mike Nieto was playing third base and a ground ball had just gone through his legs.

Jennifer was playing right field and had already missed three balls in the inning. The Mexican team was wiping us out. I looked over at Mop sitting at the end of the bench. She was sitting with her head back, looking up at the sky. Coach had taken her out of the game in the second inning.

Everybody could see that something was wrong with Mop. Coach sat next to her on the bench.

"You just weren't doing well," Coach said.

"Then I guess you had to get somebody to replace me," Mop said.

"I guess I did," Coach said.

Mop moved down the bench.

When the inning was over, Moondance came over and sat next to me. "We're going to lose and it's not even fun," he said.

"I know," I answered. "And we only have three more outs."

"Is Coach mad?"

"I think everybody is mad," I said. Chrissie was standing near the fence, fixing her hair. Her brother was standing outside the fence and talking to her. He went to college and I wondered if he was using big words. It wasn't polite to listen, but I got up to get some water and the water just happened to be near them.

"I think your team stinks," he was saying.

"It's only a stupid extra tournament," Chrissie said. "When we play in the regular season we'll win."

"You won't have momentum," her brother said. "You got to have momentum going into the season."

"So then we'll lose," Chrissie said with a shrug. Then she walked away and sat on the bench next to Mop. Things were really looking bad.

It's funny, but winning and losing makes playing ball so different. If you like playing baseball a lot, then you can have fun playing ball, but if you like winning more than you like playing ball, then it can take the fun out of playing. I think that most of our team liked playing, but people like Mr. Treaster made winning so important that it made things different.

Our first guy up in the sixth inning was Mike,

and he struck out. Then Brian got out and he hit a line drive, but the Hermanos' first baseman made a diving catch. I didn't think he saw the ball. Maybe he just heard it. That's the way that submarines find out where things are. I was going to have to try that.

Gregory got up next. He swung at the first pitch and missed. Then he swung at the second pitch and missed that one too.

Then he started waving the bat at the pitcher. He swung so hard at the next pitch it wasn't funny. He even fell down. He had struck out.

Gregory slammed the bat down and just walked off the field.

"Greg!" Coach called after him, but he just kept walking.

We watched him for a while and then started lining up. We had to line up and give the Hermanos high fives. That's what everybody did.

"I don't think Gregory is going to play next game," Coach said.

When she said that Mop got out of the line and went over and sat down on the bench. Coach watched her and then took a deep breath and turned back to shake hands with the Hermanos' coach.

After the game we all had to sit on the bench and wait for Coach to talk to us. Everybody knew she was going to be mad. Some of the Hermanos came by and made faces at us. Jennifer threw a paper cup at one of the Hermanos and he hit it with his bat.

"That's a better hit than your whole team got!" he said.

When all the Hermanos had left, Coach came and stood in front of us. Nobody wanted to look at her.

"Two things," she said. "First thing is that I'm not particularly proud of anyone's performance this game. And that goes especially for Greg."

"Greg's not here," Evans said.

"I know that," Coach said. "He should be here. The shaking hands or high-fives at the end of the game is part of sportsmanship. He lost his temper and that is not the way we do things. If he keeps that up, he won't be on the team.

"Look, guys, the Mexican team is going to win this tournament," Coach said. "But we have a chance to have the best record of the American teams. We have three wins and the Eagles have two. If they beat us, then we'll both have three wins, but they'll get to go to Japan because they scored the most runs. If we beat them, then we get to go. It's as simple as that."

When everybody started going off I saw Mop still sitting on the bench. Coach went over to talk to her, and put her arm around her. Mop tucked her head under her mom's arm, and that looked nice. I looked over at the stands to see if my mom was still there, and I saw that she was. She smiled at me and waved and I waved back. She looked really happy and I wondered if she was thinking about the baby.

Mop came over and hit me with her catcher's mask. For Mop that's pretty mushy.

"Check you dudes out later," she said.

We watched her go across the field. She was okay. Really.

"We should go and talk to Greg too," Moondance said.

"I don't know where he lives," I said. "Remember the other day when Mop asked us to go and get a soda with her?"

"We went to her house and had ice cream," Moondance said.

"You didn't tell me that."

"You didn't ask me," Moondance said with this stupid smile on.

"Yeah, well, I got Greg's address from Coach and went to his house. Only, there wasn't any house there."

"His house is gone?"

"No, I think he just doesn't live there," I said. "Maybe he doesn't want anyone to know where he lives."

"Twice I saw him go through the woods at the end of the outfield," Moondance said. "We can go through there and see where we come out. Then

we can ask people around there if they know where
he lives."

That was a good idea. I couldn't figure where
Moondance could get a good idea like that. I could
see me getting a good idea like that, but not Moondance.

Anyway, we just started walking across the outfield toward where Moondance had seen Greg go.

"I bet Greg's still going to be mad," I said. We
had reached the trees. "I'd like to be friends with
him, but he is kind of funny. What are we going to
do if he's still mad?"

"I don't know." Moondance stopped. "Can you
think of something?"

I already had thought of something. I wanted to
leave. But I didn't want to tell Moondance that I
wanted to leave. Then I thought maybe we
wouldn't find Greg. That sounded pretty good.

We started walking along a small trail through
the trees. The woods were a little bigger than I had
figured.

"Maybe we ought to walk close together," I said.

"Yeah," he answered. We walked really close together.

We went for a while longer and then Moondance
stopped. He stopped quick, like he had seen something.

"What is it?" I whispered.

"Look."

I looked over his shoulder. I could hardly see anything. We moved forward a little and then I saw what Moondance had seen.

At first it just looked like a pile of cardboard boxes. There were some branches almost covering them. We heard a noise and Moondance stepped backward. Something was coming out of the boxes. I held my breath. It was Greg.

"Hey, what are you doing in those boxes?" Moondance asked.

We started toward him. Gregory stepped toward us with his fists balled up and a really mad look on his face.

"Get out of here!" he said.

"You live here?" Moondance asked.

"I said *get out of here!*" Greg stepped forward and pushed Moondance back really hard.

There was a movement from the boxes and a woman came out. It was the woman with the shopping cart.

"What's the matter?" she said, in this high, crackly voice. "They bothering you?"

"Get out of here!" Gregory said again. He was looking around on the ground, like he was looking for something to throw at us or something. Then he picked up a piece of a branch and held it in both of his hands.

The woman was standing on one leg, then she

switched to the other one. Then she patted Greg on the shoulder and disappeared into the boxes.

I started backing away. I saw Moondance wasn't moving and I reached over and pulled him by his shirt.

"Don't forget to show up for the game," Moondance called to him. "Don't forget, Greg."

We didn't talk on the way home. We just felt super bad about the whole thing. Greg didn't have a home. I had heard about people who didn't have homes, even seen them on television, but it was different when one of them was somebody you knew.

When we got home we went right to our room.

It was such a nice room. It was a warm room and a friendly room and I loved it. I loved it so much that I didn't ever want to leave it again.

"What are we going to do?" Moondance asked.

"I don't know," I said. I looked at my brother and saw that his eyes were shiny, the way they get just before he cries. "I'll think of something," I said.

I didn't know if I could think of something, but I felt bad looking at Moondance. He wanted me to do something, and I wanted me to do something, but I didn't know what.

ome problems I know what to do about right away. When my dad gets mad or something like that, I know I shouldn't say much to him. When my mom gets mad I should try to talk to her. Those were easy problems to work on. Because if you didn't solve them they sort of solved themselves.

Then there are other kinds of problems that you don't know how to solve. Mostly they're problems with other people doing things, like in a war. A war is bad, and all you can do is say that you wish it didn't happen, that people could be friends, or at least not try to kill each other. They keep on doing it even though you don't want them to, and you don't know how to make them stop, and it gets a little scary.

Moondance and I were feeding Dad's fish. T.J. and T.J. Jr., the two new guys, looked hungry. We were just putting the top on the tank when we heard Mom opening the front door. Mop came in. She came into the room talking about how she thought she was going to hit more home runs, and then we told her about Greg.

"How come he didn't tell us?" she said.

"When we were all at the Academy, we didn't even want to tell people we were there," I said. "Sometimes I used to tell people that my parents lived in Hoboken and I was just visiting the Academy."

"Even before you were adopted?" Mop asked.

"It was easier than answering a lot of questions about how come I didn't have parents," I said.

"Maybe we should tell somebody," Moondance said.

"Then what's going to happen?" Mop asked.

That's what we didn't know. What we did know was that most of the kids at the Academy, which was where me, Mop, and Moondance had been before we got adopted, had real parents somewhere.

"Remember what Titi told us that time?" I said. "About how sometimes kids get taken away from their parents?"

"Yeah," Mop said. "I remember."

"I don't remember," Moondance said.

"You were too little," I said. "But we had a kid come in one time, I think his name was Eddie—"

"Snotty Eddie, we used to call him," Mop said.

"Yeah," I said. "He didn't even have to have a cold to have a snotty nose. Anyway, some people came to see him at the Academy and he said they were his parents. We asked how come if he had parents he was at the Academy. Titi said that sometimes, if the courts figured your folks couldn't take care of you, they took you away and put you into someplace like the Academy."

"You think that somebody might put Greg into the Academy?" Moondance asked.

I hoped that Mop would say something, but she didn't. I just shrugged.

"Let's just think as hard as we can," Mop said. "I don't want to just turn it over to grown-ups."

"We can think a lot," I said. "But we gotta do something too. It's dangerous living in the park."

Mop said she had to leave, but she would call us if she thought of anything.

Moondance went to bed pretty soon after Mop left. I was tired and not tired at the same time. I went and looked at my father's fish for a while. Being a fish looked cool. They didn't seem to think much or worry about much. It had to be more fun being a people than being a fish, but it was a lot more trouble too.

Mom asked me if I wanted some ice cream before I went to bed. Dad was out helping a friend move to a new apartment and Moondance was in bed, so just me and her were up. I said yes and she told me to get it out of the freezer.

"I think a friend of mine has a problem," I said.

"Your friends always have problems," she said.

She had this big smile on her face like it was funny or something. I don't know what she thought was so funny. Her smiling like that made me kind of mad and I kind of dropped the ice cream on the table.

"Are you annoyed about something?" she asked me in this high voice.

"Why are you smiling when I said my friend had a problem?" I asked.

"Because I felt like smiling," she said.

I think she got mad because I got mad and then she said she didn't want any ice cream and I said I didn't want any ice cream, either, so I just went to bed.

It took forever to fall asleep. I was just lying in the dark and thinking about Greg. And while I was lying there I started thinking about him lying somewhere in the dark, maybe in the park. Maybe he could hear his mother breathing the same way I could hear Moondance. Then I thought about the picnic at the park, how much food we had and even played games with the popcorn.

When I was at the Academy, hoping that someone would adopt me and Moondance, and Mop, too, because we really liked her, I used to think that life wasn't very fair. It still wasn't.

* * *

The phone rang in the morning when I was eating breakfast.

"It's Mop," Mom said.

I answered the phone in the living room. "What's up?" I asked.

"That Japanese kid called me," Mop said. "He told me not to forget about meeting him in the park. He talked like a real turkey!"

"I forgot about that guy," I said. "But suppose we can't get Four Times Seven?"

"We gotta get him," Mop said. "It's a matter of goodwill and all that."

"How do you figure that?"

"If we can't get Four Times Seven then I'll have to break his head," Mop said. "That could get the Japanese government upset or something."

"Okay," I said. "Come past the house and we'll go over to Bergen. You think any more about you know what?"

"No," Mop said softly. "You?"

"No," I answered. "See you later."

As I finished breakfast I noticed Mom wasn't talking to me very much. Then I remembered she had been mad before. So I asked her was she mad at me and she said no. I was going to say I wasn't mad anymore, either, but I forgot why I had been mad, so I didn't say anything in case I was still going to be mad if I remembered it.

Mop came up and we had to wait until she had

some breakfast. Then the three of us split over to Bergen Avenue.

Last year when we needed some help this guy named Peaches had helped us. Peaches didn't have a regular job. Sometimes he worked at the supermarket, and sometimes he worked in a used-car place. But he knew everything about the neighborhood. It was Peaches who had got Four Times Seven for us. We went over to the barbershop where Peaches hung out sometimes when he wasn't working. We found him sitting in the back of the shop playing checkers with a guy that might have been two hundred years old.

"Peaches!" Mop went up to him. "We gotta get Four Times Seven!"

"You kids in trouble again?" Peaches hadn't had much hair last year and now the top of his head was nearly bald. I don't know why he hung out in a barbershop.

"This kid said he's going to flatten me," Mop said. "I think he's a sumo wrestler or something."

"A what?" The old checker player looked at Mop. "I hope you didn't say he was no sumo wrestler!"

"That's what she said," Moondance said.

"He a Japanese?" the guy asked.

"Yeah."

"This here's Slow Willie," Peaches said. "He used to be a merchant seaman. Been all over the world."

"I seen a sumo wrestler in Osaka once," Slow

Willie said. "He must have weighed three hundred pounds. They had one of them horse and wagons— it was just a show thing—anyway, the horse got away.

"That horse started running down the street and people were just running this way and that way. You know they ain't got a lot of horses over in that part of the world. This sumo jumped out in the street and the horse tried to swerve around him. He caught that horse and pulled him down to the ground the same way you pull down a little dog or something. You can't mess with no sumo wrestler, girl."

"This a full-grown man after you, girl?" Peaches asked.

"No," Mop said. "He's a kid, but he's a strong kid."

"You can't even mess with no boy sumo wrestler," Slow Willie said.

"C'mon, let's go see Miss Sally," Peaches said.

Slow Willie went with Peaches and the rest of us.

"I don't know," he said. "I can't imagine no little cat beating no sumo wrestler."

"What little cat you talking about?" Peaches said, shaking his head. "Four Times Seven is the baddest cat in the world. He went up against a pit bull in Baltimore. The pit bull took one look at Four Times Seven and had a heart attack. He walking around Baltimore now with a pacemaker in his chest. All you got to do is sneak up behind him and say Four Times Seven and he roll over and pass out. Four Times Seven done already killed a rattlesnake in Louisiana, a mountain lion in Montana, and a armadillo in Arizona!"

"Where this cat come from?" Slow Willie had his head over to one side.

"Nobody know where he come from," Peaches said. "All they know is that somebody killed the man what owned him up in Alaska. When he did that, Four Times Seven tracked him down to Alabama."

"He tracked him from Alaska to Alabama?"

"Yeah, but by that time the man knew he was on his trail. The man got scared and turned himself in to prison and begged them for solitary confinement. Four Times Seven found the prison he was in and chewed through the concrete walls to get at him. That's how he lost all his teeth."

"He ain't got no teeth?"

"He almost got the guy, but the guy slipped away and ran into the room where they kept the electric chair. He electrocuted hisself 'cause he didn't want to face Four Times Seven."

"I don't believe a word of it," Slow Willie said.

Miss Sally lived down from the firehouse on Duncan Avenue. When Peaches rang her bell she came to the door in her housecoat.

"We need to borrow Four Times Seven," Peaches said.

Miss Sally looked us over, and then turned back to Peaches. "Four Times Seven is retired," she said. "He don't go out on calls."

"I'm *desperate*," Mop said. "We gotta have him one more time."

"Well . . ." Miss Sally took a deep breath.

"It's for the kids, Miss Sally," Peaches said.

"I don't know," Miss Sally said. "I need to be thinking about finding somebody to paint my kitchen, not worrying about how you-all treating Four Times Seven."

"You paying to have your kitchen painted?" Peaches asked.

"Sure, I'm paying," Miss Sally said. "Forty dollars."

"Then soon's we get back with Four Times Seven I'll start in on your kitchen."

"Well, you should have said that in the first place," Miss Sally said. "I'll go get Four Times Seven."

She closed the door.

"I've been all over the world," Slow Willie said, "but I've never seen no cat beat no sumo wrestler."

Just then Miss Sally opened the door and brought out Four Times Seven. He was sitting in a shopping cart with a wire cover over it so he couldn't get out. I took a step backward.

Four Times Seven had to be the ugliest cat in the whole world. Maybe even the whole universe. Part of his tail and one ear were missing. He also had chunks of hair missing. He was mostly a dirty gray with some streaks of black near his neck. Peaches was right, he didn't have any teeth, but he had these really red gums that you could see because his lips curled away in a look that was something like a smile and something like maybe he was mad. He just sat in the shopping cart and hissed.

"Now, don't keep him out all day," Miss Sally said.

"No, ma'am," Mop said.

We started toward the park. Mop led the way with me and Moondance behind her and Peaches after us pulling the shopping cart. Slow Willie was bringing up the rear.

"Have you really been around the whole world?" I asked him.

"Five times!" Slow Willie spread the fingers of his hand in front of my face. "Seen just about everything there is to be seen."

"Guess you know a lot," I said.

"Guess I do," he said.

"What would you do if you had a friend who had a problem and couldn't figure out what to do about it," I said.

"You mean like a fight with a sumo wrestler kid?" he asked.

"No, like a real hard problem," I said. "Like a kid you know, but you don't want to tell anybody his name, doesn't have a house to live in."

Slow Willie stopped and looked at me. "The best things on this earth is human beings who help each other," he said. "And the worse things on this earth is human beings who don't. Which is you?"

"But I don't know what to do," I said.

"You told me the problem," Slow Willie said. "Maybe you can tell somebody else the name."

I knew I could. I ran over to Mop and told her I had to leave.

"Not now!" she kind of screeched at me.

"Moondance will stay," I said, and I started running home.

was scared when I got home. Not scared like when I was going to get into a fight, but scared like when I had to take a big test in school. Mom wasn't home and I went right to the kitchen telephone. All the important telephone numbers were taped on the wall over the phone and I checked it carefully before I called.

A guy answered the phone and I told him who I was and that I wanted to speak to Dad. He said okay and in a minute Dad was on the phone. He asked me what I wanted.

"A friend of mine is in a lot of trouble, I think," I said.

"What kind of trouble?" he asked.

"You sound different on the phone," I said.

"What *kind* of trouble," he said, sounding more like he sounds at home.

"Remember I told you about the new kid on the team?" I asked.

"Yes?"

"I think he and his mother sleep in the park," I said. "Back in the woods behind left field."

"Going toward the highway?" he said.

"Yeah . . . you said I should tell you if I was in trouble or anything," I said. "I'm not in trouble, but I think my friend is."

He didn't say anything, but I heard him breathing on the phone. I knew he was thinking. Sometimes when he thinks, his eyes go back and forth like he's looking at something inside of him.

"How did you find where he's sleeping?" Dad said.

"Moondance saw him go into the woods a couple of times," I said. "And we went in where we always saw him go. He's not going to get into trouble, is he?"

"No," Dad said. "Look, is your mother there?"

"No."

"How you doing? You feeling okay?"

"Yeah," I said. "I guess I am."

He said he had some things to do, and for me not to worry or anything.

I waited until the end of two cartoon shows and Dad still didn't come home. I knew Mop and Moondance were probably wondering where I was, so I went back downstairs and headed toward the park. When I reached West Side Avenue I saw Mop, Slow Willie, and Peaches coming out of the park.

"Boy, that cat is really something else!" Slow Willie was shaking his head.

"Where's Moondance?"

"He went looking for you to tell you what happened," Mop said.

"So what happened?"

"Akiro came after me!" Mop said. "His eyes were bloodshot and everything!"

"He looked like a nice little boy to me," Peaches said.

"There were some other guys there from the Japanese team and they started clapping and old Akiro was coming closer and closer!" Mop's eyes got wider and her voice was whispery.

"What was Four Times Seven doing?"

"He was watching him every minute," Mop said. "He was waiting for just the right minute. Then Akiro came right at me!"

"I think that little boy was more scared than she was," Slow Willie said.

"He wasn't scared," Mop said. "That's just the way sumo wrestlers look when they're getting ready to fight. But it didn't do him any good, because Four Times Seven jumped on him."

"That little boy didn't know what hit him," Slow Willie said. "He fell backward and that cat jumped up in his face."

"He was biting his face!" Mop said.

"Only, he don't have any teeth," Peaches said.

Peaches was smiling and he didn't have many teeth either.

"If I hadn't told Peaches and Slow Willie to pull Four Times Seven off, he'd have killed him!" Mop said.

"That boy's going to dream about cat slobber for the next ten years!" Peaches said.

Slow Willie and Peaches said that they were going to take Four Times Seven home. I looked at the big gray cat and he looked happy with himself. He wrinkled up his big ugly face into what almost looked like a big ugly smile and crossed his paws as Peaches wheeled him across the street toward his home.

"Were you really scared?" I asked Mop as we went down the block.

"Sure I was," Mop said. "You know what a sumo wrestler can do to you? I mean, do you know what those guys can do?"

"Yeah, I guess," I said.

"And where did you go?" Mop asked. "I figured you had to go to the bathroom or something."

"To tell my dad about Gregory," I said. "I've been thinking about it and thinking about it, and I knew if I didn't do it right away I probably wouldn't do it at all."

"What did you do?" Mop stopped and looked at me. Her face looked serious and I wished it didn't. I wished there was something funny I could say.

"I told Dad about Greg and his mother living in the park," I said.

"Oh." Mop looked at me and then turned away.

One of the things you never did at the Dominican Academy was to do anything to get another kid in trouble. Sometimes it seemed like all the kids at the Academy were in trouble already, like we were born that way and didn't need any more.

"You think I shouldn't have done it?" I asked her.

She just shrugged, and I felt terrible. I walked Mop to her house without talking too much, and then I came home. Telling my dad seemed to be the right thing to do when I did it, but now I wasn't sure.

When I got to our apartment Mom was sitting at the table. She was crying. I didn't know what to do. There was music coming from a radio in another room. Then I saw Dinky, Moondance's toy bear, in the garbage. My brother had had the bear as long as I can remember.

"Mom?" I took Dinky out of the garbage and held him up.

"Your brother's upset," she said.

"What happened?"

"You called your father today?"

"Yes. It was about Greg, the new guy on the team."

"Your father went to the park, where Greg has

been staying," Mom said. "Then he went to the Office of Child Welfare."

"What did they say?"

"I'm afraid Greg is going to be in a children's shelter for a while."

I sat down at the other end of the table. Mom was looking at me. Her lower lip was tight and there were little dimples in it.

"Did Dad tell Moondance?"

"No," Mom said. "I did. He was very upset. I didn't know what to do and I saw Dinky lying on the counter and handed it to him."

"Moondance put Dinky in the garbage?"

She nodded. "He's mad at me, and he's mad at your father. He might even be mad at you. I don't think he's mad at us for anything we did. Just for letting things like that happen."

Terrible. That's how I felt. It wasn't just for Greg. I felt bad for Greg, but I felt bad for me too. Things shouldn't be that way. Everybody should have a home, and a family. Maybe everybody wasn't great in everything, but everybody was good enough to have a home.

"It just isn't fair," I said.

"Sometimes life is like that," Mom said. "But I think your father did the right thing, and I know you did the right thing."

"Will Greg be adopted?" I asked.

"I don't think it'll get to that," Mom said. "Your

father met his mother and she's . . . well, they're homeless, but she's really bright. She's just down on her luck right now."

"Did they do something bad?"

"Bad? No."

"Then how come they don't have a home?"

"I don't know the details, but I know they didn't do anything bad," Mom said. "You don't have to do something bad to be homeless. Sometimes . . . sometimes things just happen."

We sat for a while and I asked Mom if Dad was home and she said no. I didn't like it when Mom was sad, in fact I just about hated it. I went into my room to see what Moondance was doing.

He was lying on the bed with his face to the wall. I sat on the bed and put my hand on his shoulder and he pushed it off.

"Don't be mad at me, please," I said. "Please."

"I'm not mad," he said. "Just scared for Greg."

Dad came home for a while and then left again. I asked Mom what he was doing and she said she wasn't sure.

"He's trying to figure out what is going to be the best thing for everybody," she said.

"Maybe Greg could live with us," Moondance said.

"I don't think so," Mom said. "Especially with a new baby coming."

We went to bed kind of early and Moondance

told me again about Four Times Seven. He said one of the Japanese kids was really laughing, so he didn't think they were too mad.

In the morning I heard voices coming from the kitchen, it was Mom and Dad and Coach too. A few seconds later Dad and Coach came to the door. Mop was with them.

"We have a game today, lazyheads," Mop said.

"What happened about Greg?" I asked.

"We called the shelter," Coach said. "And asked if Greg could play today and they said he could if he wanted to, but he doesn't want to play."

"I thought we could go over and talk to him," Dad said. "Maybe we can convince him to play."

"I don't think it's going to work," Mop said.

"Maybe if the kids went over by themselves," Mom said.

"I don't want to go over," I said.

"It'll be better for Greg if he doesn't think he's been deserted," Coach said.

"I still don't want to go," I said. I didn't want to, but I was crying. Mop was still standing in the doorway and Mom was inside the room.

"T.J." Dad looked right at me. "You did the right thing. Anybody could have done nothing. You did the right thing, but the right thing isn't always easy. But easy or hard it's still right. It's still right, son."

When I stood up I felt as if my knees couldn't stay straight.

"You coming?" I put my hand on Moondance's shoulder.

He didn't move.

"We've got to get to the ballpark," Coach said. "We should get a move on."

I took a deep breath and we started toward the kitchen. Mom went into the bathroom and pulled me in. She wet a washcloth and wiped my face. Then she kissed me. When we got out, Moondance was at the door.

We dropped Coach and Mom off at the ballpark and then Dad drove over to the shelter. The shelter was all the way over on Grove, almost to city hall.

The building was big, with dark red bricks and gray blocks on the roof near the corners, so it looked a little like an evil castle. We went inside and it was as dark on the inside as it was on the outside. We were talking in whispers.

There was a guard and Dad asked him where the office was. He didn't say anything, just pointed down the hall.

We went where the guard pointed and found the office.

"We're looking for a Mrs. Mays," Dad said.

A tall woman with a big smile came over. "Are you Mr. Williams?"

Dad said he was and told the woman that me and Mop and Moondance wanted to talk to Greg.

"They're friends from his baseball team," Dad said.

"Okay, why don't you kids wait in this dayroom and I'll go up and bring him down," Mrs. Mays said.

Dad stayed in the office while me, Mop, and Moondance sat in what Mrs. Mays had called the dayroom. There was a television there, and some magazines. There was a Ping-Pong table against one wall. Outside there was a basketball court and a lot of kids were on it.

"I don't like this place," Mop said.

"The Academy was better," Moondance said.

What I was thinking was, suppose Greg was really mad? Then he would come and see me and maybe, if he knew it was me that caused him being here, he would start a fight or something. I was a pretty good fighter, so maybe he would only try to beat me up, and then I would beat him up. But I didn't want to beat him up.

"And here's Greg!" Mrs. Mays said. She still had the big smile on her face. Then she left.

Greg didn't look at us. Instead he walked over to the window and looked out at the playground.

"I told my dad about you living in the park," I said. It came out so fast, I didn't even know it was going to.

He didn't turn his head to me, just moved his eyes over and looked at me. I felt a little scared, but not too scared. Then he looked down at the play-ground again.

"I'm sorry," I said.

He didn't say anything.

"You going to play with us today?" Mop asked.

"Why would I want to play with your old rag-gedy team?" he asked.

"Thought you wanted to play," Mop said.

"Get out of here," he said.

"If you don't play," I said, "we might lose."

"Good," he said, almost to himself.

"If you want us to lose, then we don't want you to play," Mop said.

"You hate us?" Moondance asked.

Greg pushed back the curtain from the window so that he could see a little better. "I don't hate nobody," he said. "I just gotta be thinking what I'm going to do. Can't waste my time playing baseball."

"I do some of my best thinking playing baseball," I said.

"And we can use another good batter," Mop said. "Come on, man."

Greg turned toward us and spit on the ground. "Why don't you just leave us alone!" he said. "Why'd you have to start all this mess?"

"Where's your mom?" I asked.

"How do I know?" he asked. "I don't even care where she is. I wish I didn't know where you were, either."

He stepped toward me and I walked away from him and out of the room.

"T.J.!" Mop was calling me.

I went back to the office where Dad was waiting. He was sitting and talking to Mrs. Mays and they both stood up when they saw me coming.

"Does he want to play ball?" Dad asked.

"No, but I think he wants to know if his mother is okay," I said.

"We told him that she's going to be okay," Mrs. Mays said.

"Can she come and watch him play ball?" I asked.

"Well, we don't have anything to do with that but . . ." Mrs. Mays shook her head as if she were agreeing with something she had said to herself. "I'll see to it that she can," she said.

I went back to the dayroom. Mop and Moondance were alone in the middle of the room and Greg was still near the window.

"Hey, Greg, your mom's coming to the game," I called to him. "She probably wants to see you play."

He turned and looked at me. "I don't want her there," he said.

"Then you'd better get to the game and tell her yourself," I said.

We stood for a minute, and then Mop turned and started walking out. Moondance started after her, then me. I stopped at the door and turned to see if

Greg was coming. He was still standing at the window.

"Come on," I called to him. "We're going to be late."

He gave me a look, but he came.

Dad had Greg's uniform and handed it to him as we got into the car. We got to the game just as the Elks were taking the field. There were more people at the game than I had ever seen before. It looked like half the city was there. Brian had on the catching gear and Coach called time out so Mop could put it on and catch. Greg sat on the end of the bench. I looked around, but I didn't see his mother.

Mr. Treaster was really mad. He started yelling at the umpire for giving Mop time to put her gear on, but nobody seemed to care.

Brian was pitching and not doing too good. Before we could look twice, the Eagles had the bases loaded.

"T.J., get your brother warmed up," Coach said.

I didn't want to warm Moondance up because he threw too hard. I've got little bones in my hands, which makes them hurt when you throw the ball too hard. Also, I have those lines on my palms that tell you where the nerves go. When the ball hits one of those lines, the pain goes right along them up my arm.

I thought Coach was going to say something to

Greg, but she didn't. She just looked at him and nodded like it wasn't even a big deal. Maybe she was worried about the game. If we beat the Eagles we could get to go to Japan.

The game started again and this big kid named Dennis was up for the Eagles. He hit a ball straight up in the air. You couldn't even see it, that's how far it went up. But when it came down, guess who was under it and caught it? Mop!

She looked over at Mr. Treaster and smiled, and he wrote something down on his clipboard so hard he broke his pencil.

Then the next batter hit a ground ball right at Brian. He got it, tagged the runner out, and threw to first and hit Chrissie right on the knee!

Chrissie went down on the ground and started rolling around and screaming and the umpire called another time out. Mr. Testor, Chrissie's father, came over and looked at her knee and said it was all right. Mrs. Testor was there, too, and she wanted to talk to Chrissie, but Mr. Testor wouldn't let her. Mrs. Testor looked worried.

The Eagles had scored one run. Then Chris Baber struck out and we were up.

Phffft! Phffft! Phffft!

That's how the ball sounded when Rocky pitched it. Chrissie, Mike, and Mop all struck out. Then the Eagles were up again.

Moondance was still warming up.

"Don't throw it toward my face!" I called to him.

"T.J., wear the mask," Titi yelled.

"I got it on!" I called back to Titi.

It was just as bad catching with the mask on as it was with the mask off. If you missed the ball, it always hit your shoulders and arms and things. Usually it didn't hit your face because you moved your head out of the way if you saw the ball coming too close to your face.

The first two Eagles made easy outs. Then the next guy hit a hard ground ball right at Mike on third base.

You wouldn't believe what the ball did. First it bounced off the ground and hit Mike in the chest and then it went straight up into the air. Mike watched it and caught it on the way down. Then he threw to second.

But the ball went past the second baseman into right field and the runner went around second and started to third. Then the right fielder threw the ball to Joey DeLea at second. Joey got the ball and threw it to Mike at third. It hit him right in the same spot in his chest.

Mike was really mad and started chasing the ball. Everybody was yelling for the runner to go home. He started just as Mike got to the ball. Mike threw it as hard as he could and it went right over Mop's head. They had another run.

A bus came, the kind that takes kids to school.

Only, instead of kids it had a lot of older women and some older guys in it.

"T.J.," Coach called to me. "Keep warming up Moondance!"

"Look!" Mrs. Mays was getting off the bus and I thought I recognized one of the women getting off with her.

Coach turned and looked. We all looked and it was true, it was Mrs. Mays and Greg's mom together. I looked over at Greg and he gave me a mean look.

His mom looked pretty nice. She was fixed up and everything and you couldn't tell that she had been living in the park. She just looked like a regular person.

"T.J.!" Coach yelled at me again.

I don't like being yelled at. That's probably why I missed the next ball and it hit me right on the thumb. A big scream was going to come out of me, but then I remembered Dad was there.

I looked over to see if he was looking, but he was looking at Mom.

"Ooowweee!" The thumb hurt something terrible.

The next guy on the Eagles made an out. Then our guys got up.

Phffft! Phffft! Phffft!

Brian, Joey, and Evans struck out. The end of two innings and the score was two to nothing in favor of the Eagles.

The ice cream truck was right behind the Eagles' dugout and some of the mothers were buying sodas and ice creams for them.

"We need some sodas," Evans said.

"We need to keep our minds on the game," Coach said.

"If I had a soda I could keep my mind on the game more," Evans said.

Mop gave him a look and he shut up.

In the third inning the whole French team showed up. They came over to our side and started cheering for us. Stefan was near where I was warming up Moondance.

"We are number one!" he said.

Two of their guys struck out and then Rocky came up. He hit the first pitch exactly one thousand and fifteen miles and nine inches! That ball was like a missile! It would have been over the wall in Yankee Stadium.

When Rocky came around the bases the guy from the *Journal* was taking pictures. For a minute, just a minute, I imagined I was Rocky. Then I went back to being me.

When we got up in the third our first two guys struck out, then Jennifer hit a ground ball to their first baseman, which would have been a double or something, only he caught it and tagged first for the out.

Coach put in Moondance to pitch, me on third

base, and Greg in left field. Brian moved over to shortstop.

"We're losing by three runs, guys," she said. "Let's use our heads."

Moondance walked the first batter. Then he walked the second batter. Then he struck out two batters in a row. The next guy that got up hit a pop-up.

Chrissie was playing first base and the ball was coming down near her. Brian was yelling.

"She's gonna miss it! She's gonna miss it!"

Only, she didn't miss it. She caught it and then she walked over to Brian and handed it to him and he pushed her and she pushed him back. He was going to flatten her, but Titi got in between them.

Chrissie got up first and struck out. Then I got up. The first ball came by so quick, I didn't even see it. *Whack!*

"Strike one!"

"That ball hits you, you're going to be sore for about a month!" That's what their catcher said.

That was supposed to make me afraid of the ball. I wasn't afraid though, and I didn't even move when the next pitch came.

"Strike two!"

"You can't hit anyway," the catcher said. "The next ball is going to be right down the middle of the plate. You're still going to miss it."

I notice things, like Dad said. And I noticed that

their catcher always caught the ball. So what I was going to do was to look where his glove was and swing right in front of the glove.

Rocky wound up and I looked at the glove and swung.

"Strike three!"

If he hadn't moved the glove at the last minute it probably would have been a triple, that's how hard I swung. Maybe even a homer.

Mop hit a ground ball right back to their pitcher. Rocky threw it to first base for the third out.

At the end of four innings it was still Eagles three, us . . . nothing.

Top of the fifth inning. The first guy on their team struck out. The second guy struck out. Then Rocky was up.

"Come on, Moondance," Coach was calling out. "You can get him!"

Rocky hit the first pitch right past Moondance out to center field. He got all the way to second base.

"Attaboy, Rock! Attaboy!" Mr. Treaster was calling out to Rocky.

"Be ready, T.J." Mop pointed at me.

It was strike one, and when Moondance threw the next pitch Rocky took off.

"Strike two!" the umpire yelled as Mop threw the ball down to me. Rocky was sliding in to third base just as the ball reached me.

"Safe!"

"Nice catch, T.J.," Coach said.

I looked in the stands. Dad gave me the thumbs-up sign.

The batter swung on the next pitch and missed. We were getting up again.

"Let's get something started!" Brian was yelling.

I looked up in the stands and saw Greg's mother talking to another woman. She looked pretty happy up there.

Then she looked over to where Greg was sitting and waved to him. He waved back, a sort of half wave, and he looked down. I had to bend over to see his face to see if he was looking sad. He wasn't.

"What are you looking at?" he said.

I smiled at him and he looked away. Mom said they hadn't done anything wrong, and I believed her, but I still thought that Greg was feeling bad about it like he had done something wrong.

Brian got up and hit the ball on the ground into left field. He went flying into first base and all the guys on our team started giving each other high fives. Then Joey got up. The first pitch hit him right in the back.

Okay, Evans is up next. Coach touched her nose two times and her ear once. That means bunt. Soon as she did that all the Eagles moved in real close.

"They know our signals!" Coach said.

The first pitch came and Evans bunted. The

third-base guy on the Eagles came in to get it and so did their shortstop. The third-base guy got it and turned to throw to third base, only there wasn't anyone there for him to throw it to. Then he turned to throw it to first base, but there wasn't anyone there to throw it to either.

Mr. Treaster was screaming and jumping up and down, but the bases were still loaded. Greg was up.

Mr. Treaster moved all of his guys back and told them to get a double play.

"Heet it!" a French kid called out.

Mr. Treaster gave him a dirty look.

Greg missed the first ball, for strike one. Then he missed the second ball, for strike two. He didn't swing at the third ball.

"Strike three!"

Greg had his head down when he came back to the bench. Titi ran over to him and pushed his chin up. I looked to see who was up next. Moondance.

"He's all yours, Rocky!" Chris Baber called out from second base.

Moondance hit the first pitch over the third baseman's head. Everybody was screaming and jumping up and down. Brian came in to score. Then Joey came in. Then Evans came in and Moondance was on second base. Three to three!

Jennifer was up next.

The first pitch that came to Jennifer, she missed by about a foot. Maybe even two feet. Then the next ball was low and she swung at that and missed it. Mr. Treaster pointed up. Rocky nodded.

The next pitch was really high and Jennifer swung at it anyway.

Crack!

The ball went toward the outfield and Moondance started toward third.

"Get him at third! Get him at third!" Their catcher pointed at Moondance.

I was watching the ball. It went farther and farther. I looked down to see their left fielder. First he was moving back slowly and hitting his glove with his fist. Then he started running back. Then he jumped, but the ball was over his glove and hit the fence. It started rolling back toward the infield.

Moondance came in to score and Jennifer was tearing around the bases.

"Run!" Coach was screaming and jumping up and down.

Mop grabbed her and made her sit down, but she got up again as Jennifer got to third. It was a triple and we were winning, four to three.

Okay, so Coach was crying and Mop was trying to calm her down.

Next up was Chrissie. She hit a ground ball to third base and was out at first.

I was up next. I got my first good hit. If their shortstop hadn't been playing almost in the outfield it would have been an easy double. Maybe, if it had rolled all the way to the fence, it could have been a home run. Anyway, their shortstop was lucky to catch it. That's what I think.

It was the top of the sixth inning and we were winning. I was really nervous. I wanted to win, but mainly I didn't want to be the one to mess up.

Their left fielder was up first and Moondance struck him out. Mop was yelling at everybody. Saying things like "Be ready!" and "Look alive!"

I kept my eyes as wide as I could so I wouldn't miss anything.

Their first batter missed the first two pitches. Mr. Treaster was yelling at him to keep his eye on the ball.

"What are you swinging at, anyway?" he yelled. "That ball was outside!"

The batter didn't swing at the next pitch and the umpire called it a ball. It was one ball and two strikes.

The guy hit the next pitch right back at Moondance. He knocked it down with his bare hand and threw it to first base. Two outs!

But Moondance was hopping around and shaking his hand. Coach called time out and went out to see him. We all did. He was crying and holding his pitching hand where the ball had hit it.

"Get some ice," Titi called.

We got ice and put it on Moondance's hand.

Coach put her arm around him and told Brian to pitch. Moondance was out of the game.

"We just need one more out!" Mop was saying. "Everybody hold up one finger!"

We all held up one finger. One more out. Up in the stands the women who came in the bus were holding up one finger. Then the French team was doing it.

"One run ties it up!" Mr. Treaster yelled out. "Just one run ties it up!"

Brian started pitching. He hit the first guy he faced. Then he hit the second guy. Then he threw the next ball into the ground. Mop went out to the mound and called the infield in.

"What's the matter with you?" Mop said.

"Nothing!" Brian said. He looked nervous.

"Then throw strikes!" Mop said.

The next pitch went into the dirt and Mop just managed to catch it. The next ball was high. So was the next ball. They had the bases loaded.

I was a little scared. Not too scared, but a little. Coach went out to Brian.

"Just toss it over the plate," Coach said. "Make the next batter swing. Okay?"

Brian nodded.

He threw the first pitch so soft that you could have caught it with your bare hands.

"Strike one!"

"Give it a ride!" the Eagles were calling out.

"Strike two!" Another easy pitch.

Mop ran out and said something to Brian, then ran back behind the plate.

Brian looked in, and then threw the ball as hard as he could.

Crack! It was a hard smash to Joey DeLea. Joey dove for the ball, but it went right past him to the outfield. Before you knew it they had scored two runs and we were behind again. Everybody felt terrible, just terrible.

Their next batter popped up and Brian caught it. But they were ahead, five to four.

"Just make contact with the ball," Coach was saying. "Don't try to hit a home run. Just make contact!"

Mop was up first. She hit the first ball right over Rocky's head into the outfield.

"Play for two! Play for two!" Mr. Treaster called out. He wanted the Eagles to get a double play.

Brian was up next and he hit the first pitch straight up into the air. Their catcher caught it and that was one out.

"C'mon, Joey!" Everybody was yelling. Joey wiggled the bat like he was going to kill the ball. Then he struck out. Two outs.

Evans was up next.

"Evans, be patient!" Coach called out.

The first pitch was in the dirt. Evans swung and

missed. The next pitch was in the dirt too. Evans swung again. Strike two!

"One more, baby!" Mr. Treaster called out.

All the Eagles were standing up and cheering.

"Rocky!" Mr. Treaster looked at his pitcher and held his hands apart.

"He wants to make sure that Rocky throws Evans a bad pitch to swing at," Coach said. She looked miserable.

It was a bad pitch all right. It hit Evans right on the top of his head. Evans shook his fist at Rocky, but the umpire got in between them. Then Evans went to first base and Greg was up.

"Hey, you need a pinch hitter for that kid!" somebody yelled from the stands.

"You can do it, Greg," Chrissie said really softly.

"He can't hear that," I said. "Yell it out!"

"You can do it, Greg!" We both yelled.

"Strike one!" The first pitch didn't even look close, but the umpire called it a strike.

"Strike two!" Greg had swung and missed.

Greg stepped out of the batter's box and looked over at us. Coach clapped her hands and gave him the thumbs-up sign.

The next ball was really close and he didn't swing.

"Ball!"

Mr. Treaster dropped his clipboard and stared at the umpire. Then he shook his head.

Rocky wound up and pitched. Greg swung and the ball went toward the outfield. Everybody stood up. I held my breath. We watched the ball go and go. Their outfielder didn't even move. He just watched the ball come out to him and then turned as it went over his head. It was over his head and over the fence. A home run! Three runs scored. We had won!

Jumping around? You never saw so much jumping around unless you saw us jumping around. We got into a big pile on the field and everybody jumped on. The French team came and jumped on us. Some of them jumped on some of the Eagles, too, which almost started a fight. And right on the bottom of the pile was Greg. And he was saying things like "You'd better get off of me or I'll knock you out!" but he couldn't even say it good because we were all over him. We had won our biggest game and it was really good. Maybe I'm just a winner.

ad went and got the paper the next day and there was only one small little story about the game. It said that Mr. Treaster's team enjoyed the tournament and that the Mexican team won, but that it was only a warm-up for the regular season.

Greg turned out to be half an orphan. His father had died and he lived with his mom. I heard Coach telling my mom that she could do a lot of things, like type and answer telephones and that kind of stuff. Coach also said that she had a head for numbers too. Now, that was kind of funny, because I imagined her having this really weird head with little numbers sticking out of it. If people have heads for things I probably have a head for baseball, which is why I play so good.

Some people from the mayor's office found a place for Greg and his mother, but it wasn't that good. Me, Moondance, and Mop went over to see him and he wasn't doing that good.

"You don't like your new place?" Moondance asked.

"It's okay," Greg said. "But I don't know what's going to happen next or nothing like that. You're too dumb to know about stuff like that."

I didn't mind him saying that, because he always talks kind of tough, that's just the way Greg is. But he was wrong about us not knowing what it was like to not know what was going to happen next. One day me and Moondance and Mop were going have to tell him about waiting to get adopted.

Later Greg's mom lost her job and Sister Titi arranged for her to live at the Academy until she found some other work. Then she got a regular job and a part-time job working at a restaurant.

"How's she going to have any time for herself if she has to work on two jobs?" Moondance asked.

"She won't for a while," Dad said. "But right now she just wants to get their lives in order, and I think she's really glad to have the two jobs. They'll be okay, but it won't be easy. At least they have a chance."

I didn't think it was that hard just to be okay, to have a home and enough to eat and stuff like that. The funny thing was that you couldn't just look at Greg and know that he was having a hard time. People look the same and you sort of figure if you're doing okay, then they must be doing okay too.

Another thing I thought about was the Nagasaki Knights. When we said good-bye to them, Akiro was laughing about Four Times Seven as much as we were. But I remember what Mom had said about maybe the grandparents of the Japanese team being in the war and being bombed and all. I didn't know how that could have happened, how nice guys like the Knights could be in a war.

"How come bad things like that happen?" I asked Mom.

"I'm not really sure," Mom said.

"Maybe we have to watch out for each other more," I said.

"I think that would help a lot," she said.

I hope she's right because I know I can do that.

Oh, yes. By now Mom looks like she's really going to have a baby. She doesn't come to practice most of the time, and when she does come Moondance always stays right next to her.

"So you don't bump her or nothing," he said.

I asked him what he wanted. What I meant was if he wanted a sister or a brother.

"Somebody friendly," he said, looking real serious. "Like me."

What I wanted was a boy who could hit and play outfield. If it was a boy I'd teach him everything I knew and then he'd be great like me if he practiced a lot. Maybe not as great as me but probably pretty good. If it turned out to be a girl, I'd let her be a catcher, like Mop, which is okay, too, because a good catcher is hard to find.